CHRISTMAS WITH CHARLIE

A NOVELLA

Carol Ervin

LIST OF CHARACTERS

Characters who are important in this and other books in the Mountain Women series, listed by first name:

Barlow Townsend: husband of May Rose, former superintendent of the Winkler Lumber Company, former partner in the Winkler Mine, now owner of Townsend's General Store

Blanche Cotton Herff: wife of Charlie, daughter of Simpson Wainwright (deceased)

Charlie Herff: ex-cowboy, brother of Will and Glory, married to Blanche

Dessie Thomas: cook in Hester's boardinghouse, now married to Tom and resident/helper in May Rose's kitchen

Freddy Townsend: son of May Rose and Barlow, a university student

Glory Townsend Bell: adopted daughter of Barlow's sister, biological sister to Will and Charlie Herff, married to Randolph Bell, mother of Johnny, owner of Glory Wear, a sewing factory

Hettie Townsend: daughter of May Rose and Barlow

Jonah Jr. Watson: son of Jonah and Bertha

May Rose (Percy) (Long) Townsend: wife of Barlow and mother of Freddy and Hettie, Wanda's stepmother

Otis: son of Wanda and Will Herff

Parker Robinson: Lou Graves's foster son

Piney Bosell Wainwright: Wanda's aunt, widow of Simpson Wainwright

Randolph Bell: engineer, married to Glory

Tom Thomas: married to Dessie, operator of Townsend Filling Station and helper in May Rose's kitchen

Wanda (Wyatt) Herff: daughter of Jamie Long and Evalena Bosell, stepdaughter of May Rose (Long) Townsend, widow of Will Herff, mother of Evie, Otis, and Wanda Rose

Wanda Rose Herff: daughter of Wanda and Will

Characters in the series, listed by first name, who may appear briefly in this story or are only mentioned.

Bertha Graves Watson: former teacher, married to Jonah Watson, sister of Lou Graves

Ebert Watson: old friend of Will's, former suitor to May Rose, grandfather of Jonah Jr.

Evalena Bosell, (deceased): Wanda's mother

Evie (Wyatt/Doddy): daughter of Wanda and Homer Wyatt (deceased), married to Lester Junior Doddy

Jamie Long (deceased): first husband of May Rose, Wanda's father

Lou Graves: widower, Bertha's brother

Russell Long (deceased): May Rose's brother-in-law from her first marriage, Wanda's uncle

Simpson Wainwright (deceased): miller and carpenter, father of Blanche, husband of Piney Bosell

Will Herff (deceased): Wanda's second husband, father of Otis and Wanda Rose, retired doctor, former partner in the Winkler Mine, artist

CHAPTER 1

There's one Christmas I recall in more detail than others because it was so different. I'm not sure of the year, but I know my children were home from the university, so it had to be after 1937, because that's when my daughter Hettie graduated from high school. It may have been the last year we were all together.

In those years before the war, Winkler was a lot smaller than it is now, with the mines still closed and only one major employer, the clothing factory owned and managed by Glory Bell, my husband's niece. In the most prosperous days of the factory, Glory employed nearly 80 women and men. But that was later, during the war, when they were making uniforms.

The success of Glory Wear, which we sometimes still called Glory's sewing shop, meant we also had electric service. The new power plant was fueled not by sawdust, as in the days when Winkler was a sawmill town, and not by coal, as in the days of the coal mines, but by oil that came to us by rail. Yes, remote as we were, trains still came to Winkler; they just didn't come every day.

Because of Glory Wear and a private investment in the electric plant, the town hadn't died when Randolph Bell's coal mine finally shut down. Our population had drastically shrunk, but we'd kept the hospital and school, our doctor had stayed with us, and there were still a few small businesses like Townsend's General Store and Townsend's Gas & Oil, both owned by Barlow, my husband.

In the years of the town's decline we'd learned to respect how our enterprises and institutions relied on each other. I was proud that their support came from people who'd risked their livelihoods and their savings to keep the community we loved from becoming one more abandoned town. Winkler was quieter in those years, and without the grit and dust of the mines it was cleaner, though it never was one of those lovely picture-postcard little towns. Still, I liked our town, because most of the people I loved were there.

The Christmas I am remembering stands out from the others because it was infused with our concerns for Charlie. He'd caused me a lot of worry over the years, starting when he'd run away from his father's home when he was about nine years old. Then when he was 15 and living with me in Fargo, he'd left to follow his dream of being a cowboy and we'd had no news of him for a decade. After he returned to Winkler and became a deputy sheriff for the county, we got used to the fact that he seldom told anyone anything about himself, not even when he was still living with his wife, Blanche. He never seemed comfortable in our homes, but though he was unsociable, he had a spirit of helpfulness. Both as a deputy and as a breeder of horses he was respected by everyone.

Charlie's family requires some explanation. His only living blood relatives were his sister Glory and her son, Johnny Bell, and Otis and Wanda Rose, the children of his deceased brother, Will Herff. As sometimes happens in poor families, Charlie, Glory and Will had not grown up together. Glory became a Townsend, adopted when she was just a toddler by Hester, my husband's spinster sister. That's why Glory was Barlow's niece though her brothers were not his nephews. Blood doesn't always make a family. The Herffs and Townsends were family for other reasons.

Charlie had come to Fargo with me, but Will had chosen to stay with their father. Years later, Will married my stepdaughter Wanda, at the time a young widow with a daughter. At the Christmas I'm thinking about now, Will had been dead several years. Once upon a time he'd saved Winkler too, but that's another story. I guess Will was our inspiration. He died too soon, but everything he did for his community was destined to last for generations.

Here's something I've learned: no matter how happy and well-known a family may be, there's always a lot of hidden sadness and a lot of hidden history.

In his way, Charlie loved us. I figured he'd lay down his life for Glory or Wanda or any of us, and he still called me "Ma," though not very often. Charlie didn't talk much unless it was about horses. I'd given up trying to understand why he wouldn't come to our family gatherings.

That year he'd promised to be with us on Christmas day, so that was different. I remember the weather was mild for December. On the last day of school before the holiday the children had run out for recess without their coats, and after school I'd driven home to the boardinghouse with the car windows rolled down, refreshed by a pleasant breeze. I remember the weather because in my mind's eye I see the young people of our family arriving home for the holidays, none of them wearing coats. It's odd how one memory triggers an image, then another memory, and so on. When so much has changed, it helps to go over our memories again and again.

At times we still referred to home as "the boardinghouse", though we hadn't taken borders for several years. The house had become the permanent home for Tom and Dessie Thomas, old friends and our former cooks. Tom now managed Townsend's Gas and Oil, so Dessie was home alone most days. With her bad knees, she had a hard time getting around, but she pitched in and did what she could.

After we stopped taking boarders, our house also became home for Wanda and her two younger children, Otis and Wanda Rose. Otis was at the university in Morgantown that year, along with our Freddy and Hettie.

Wanda Rose rode home with me, that last day of school before Christmas, but before we got there she asked me to drop her off at Piney's. I loved how dutifully Wanda Rose visited her mom's Aunt Piney, who was sweet as ever but increasingly mixed up about things.

"Look, your mother's here," I said, when I stopped our Ford in Piney's lane, for Wanda's old coupe was parked there. Wanda hurried toward us from the barn, waving her arms. When Wanda wasn't working at the hospital, she often wore Will's old shirts and pants with the cuffs rolled up and the waist bunched in with a belt. Today she also wore a long butcher's apron.

"I can't find Charlie," she said, coming to my window. "Do you know where he went?"

As usual, I did not.

"I phoned but he didn't answer," she said. "I don't know why he has a phone when he's never there to answer it. So I drove over there and saw old John Johnson in the field, breaking out bales of hay for Charlie's horses. John said Charlie went somewhere day before yesterday but was supposed to be home by nightfall. John hasn't seen him since. John said he was wearing his badge and took his rifle, so he figured the sheriff had sent him to some trouble."

I dared not imagine what kind of trouble. There was one thing Charlie never seemed to understand: because he told us nothing we worried more.

"What's happening? Is Piney okay?"

"It's that heifer," Wanda said. "Piney's as mixed up as ever, and Blanche is down sick with a cold. She phoned me about the heifer, poor thing's been trying to have her calf since yesterday. That's why we need Charlie. The calf is turned backwards."

Wanda Rose and I got out of the car and hurried after Wanda to the barn.

Wanda bent and wiped her hands on clean straw. "I put my hand in there to see if I could turn the calf. I've seen Charlie do it, but I'm not strong enough. Anyway I think now is too late to turn it. The back hooves are sticking out."

I gasped when I saw the tips of those small black hooves protruding from the heifer's backside. She was breathing hard, clearly restless and uncomfortable.

"I once saw my uncle put a chain around a calf's hooves and pull it out," I said.

"Yeah, that works fine when the front feet are coming first. This poor baby's gonna have to be pulled, but turned wrong like it is means trouble. Pulling too hard and quick could crush its ribs. Anyway the three of us together won't be strong enough to do it."

The heifer was a pretty Jersey, the breed Piney and her late husband had always favored because Jerseys gave rich milk.

"Could Dr. Madison help?"

Wanda shook her head. "I don't know if he's ever pulled a calf but I know for a fact he's tending to a lot of sick folks." She wiped her forehead with the back of her hand. "Shouldn't our kids be getting home from Morgantown about now? Otis could help, or maybe the farm boys will know what to do. One of you go home and see if you can catch them."

I hurried to my car, and Wanda Rose ran to Piney's house to alert Dessie to our current need. By "farm boys" Wanda meant Bertha and Jonah Watson's son, Jonah Jr., and Lou Graves's foster son, Parker, also students at the university. Today they were giving a ride home to Otis, Freddy, and Hettie.

CHAPTER 2

I remember how relieved and happy I was when I turned into our lane and saw that Plymouth parked in front of the house, all four doors standing open, and Otis and Freddy transferring suitcases to the porch. At that moment I wasn't thinking about the heifer and her calf. My spirits soared because I hadn't seen our young people in months.

Beside the car, Hettie and Jonah Jr. stood close in conversation. Apparently their interest in each other had not changed. I liked this young man and his family, and I felt sure Hettie would never find anyone better, but I still had trouble acknowledging that my little girl had grown-up feelings. I had no idea about my son's feelings. In matters of love, Freddy was as hard to read as his father.

I stopped my car, blocking the drive, and got out, waving both arms.

"Mom," Hettie called. "What's wrong?"

"Oh, welcome home! It's wonderful to see you, but I'm afraid we've got an emergency. Piney's heifer has a calf coming backwards and Wanda needs help to pull it. She thought some of you might have done this before."

"Lead the way," Jonah Jr. said. All of them got back in Parker's car and followed me to Piney's.

Sure enough, when they reached the barn, Jonah Jr. and Parker took charge, agreeing with Wanda that the calf had to be pulled slowly. Wanda and Otis quickly spread a thick mat of clean straw behind the heifer, because the floor was a smeary mix of mud and manure, along with blood and slime from the straining heifer.

I stood out of the way with Hettie, admiring her and the other young people, so ready for action. Hettie looked different, her face thinner. Her hair was different too, the dark ends curling on her shoulders. Her eyes looked tired, but maybe they were only anxious, focused on Jonah Jr., who'd fastened a chain on the calf's hooves. There was little I could do, and I wasn't eager to witness the poor heifer's distress, but leaving would feel like deserting the ones who were trying to help.

Jonah Jr. and Parker had rolled up their sleeves, but in their white shirts and ties, argyle sweater vests and slacks, they were dressed too nicely for this task. Never a farm boy, my Freddy stood in the open doorway, looking as uneasy as I felt. Otis and Wanda Rose stood closer, watching attentively. Both hoped to be doctors, though Wanda Rose admitted she might have a better chance of being accepted to nursing school.

"Yeah, this has to be slow and gentle," Parker said. "Can someone find a glove or a piece of leather or a stout stick to help us hold this chain?" Wanda and Otis searched a nearby workbench and found two new hammer handles. Wound in the ends of the chains, the handles offered a better grip.

"This is gonna get messy," Wanda said, taking off her apron and tying it around Parker. "May Rose, see if Piney has another apron and maybe a couple of old shirts.

I was glad to get out to fresh, open air. Piney met me at her kitchen door. In everything except comprehension, she seemed just the same, her face pretty and smooth, and her hair blond with only a few streaks of gray. Today, her hair was loose and uncombed, probably because Blanche was too sick to tend to it.

"Blanche don't feel good," she said. "Do we have company?"

"The children are home from university," I said. "They've come to help Wanda." I didn't mention the heifer's ordeal. "Wanda wants to know if we can borrow a couple of aprons or old shirts."

"There's shirts and aprons somewhere," Piney said. "Take your pick. Do you need me to help?"

"Not yet. Wait here until I come for you." I took a bib apron from a hook in the pantry and two of Simpson's old shirts from the closet in Piney's room. Back in the barn, Hettie tied the apron on Jonah Jr. and we helped him and Parker into Simpson's shirts.

It was now approaching five o'clock on the shortest day of winter and Piney's barn had no electric light. "Mother," Freddy said, lifting a rusty lantern from a nail near the door. "Can you find more of these?"

I went back to the house and asked Piney if she had lanterns somewhere. She said she didn't know.

"Is it all right if I look for them?"

"Take anything you want," she said. "Would you like cookies?"

I found two lanterns on a top shelf of Piney's pantry. She wanted to accompany me to the barn.

"It's getting dark, and someone needs to sit here and listen in case Blanche calls for help. Wait for me—I'll come for you as soon as the calf is born."

"Blanche is sick," she said.

"Yes, she can see the calf tomorrow. I won't be gone long."

In the next hour I went back and forth from the barn to the house, peeking in on Blanche and assuring Piney all was well. In the barn the heifer struggled to push the calf out, Jonah Jr. and Parker assisting gently, their feet braced in the straw, with Otis and Freddy behind them for support. Parker said sweat was running into his eyes, and Hettie stepped forward and blotted his forehead with her handkerchief.

"When we see the top of the calf's tail, we've only got a few minutes to get it out alive," Parker said. "Pop says when a calf comes backwards like this, its cord gets cut soon as the hips are free."

He and Jonah Jr. agreed with Wanda—if they pulled harder they risked crushing the calf's ribs. "The poor cow," Hettie said.

"Wait till you see she's having a contraction," Wanda said. "Then pull."

I thought I was going to faint. I closed my eyes but opened them when I heard everyone sigh in relief. The calf's chest slipped out, then right away its head, followed by its front legs. When it dropped to the ground the heifer turned and nosed it. We watched as she began to lick it. "Good," Wanda said. "A first-time ma don't always know what to do."

"It's breathing," Parker said, wiping his face with his sleeve. "Somebody see if its nose is clear."

Otis stepped forward and used his white handkerchief to clean mucus from the calf's nose.

"It's a bull calf," Wanda Rose said, proud as if she'd produced it herself.

The mother butted her head aggressively toward her helpers, who decided it would be best to leave her and her baby alone for a while.

"You-all can go to the house and have a wash," Wanda said. "I'll watch here to make sure it gets up to suck."

Inside, I re-introduced the young people to Piney. "Aunt Piney, you have a new calf," Wanda Rose said.

"I do? Does Simpson know?"

"I'm sure he does," I said. Some days Piney cried because her husband had passed away, but often she thought he was still with her, just out of sight. "Wanda Rose will take you to see it."

Before going upstairs to check on Blanche, I used Piney's

phone and called Bertha Watson, Jonah Jr.'s mother, to say we'd enlisted the help of the boys in the calf emergency and they'd soon be on their way. As an afterthought, I asked if she or Lou had seen Charlie. Lou was Bertha's brother and Parker's foster father. Charlie bought hay from Lou, who might have been the closest thing he had to a friend.

"I'll ask," Bertha said. I don't think Charlie's been around for several weeks. Are you worried?"

"He's off on deputy business but he was supposed to be back a day or two ago."

"You know Charlie," Bertha said.

"I do." Even our friends knew Charlie was unpredictable. By this time I should have learned not to worry. Still, I couldn't stop feeling like an anxious mother.

"Jonah Jr. and Parker saved Piney's heifer and her calf," I said.

"Ah, Jonah and Lou will be proud."

Bertha thanked me for letting her know the boys would soon be home. "Charlie will turn up," she said.

"I know." He always had.

CHAPTER 3

Wanda wanted to go home, have dinner with our children, and hear what Otis and the others had to tell about their college experiences. But Blanche was in no condition to watch over Piney, and we couldn't depend on Piney to help Blanche.

Wanda Rose offered to stay with Piney and fix supper for her. "Bless you," Wanda said. "I'll come back and stay the night."

Before leaving, I went upstairs to tell Blanche about the calf, but she was asleep, breathing in rasps, her face hot and dry. Other than a dress flung over a chair and shoes on the floor, the room was as neat as the rest of the house. We were proud of the way Blanche had settled down. In years gone by, she'd been less than responsible, leaving her small children and running off with their father, who didn't want them. After his death, she'd abandoned her responsibilities more than once, going off with other men.

Blanche had finally earned the family's respect by caring for Simpson and Piney, her father and stepmother, and after Simpson died, managing the house and supervising Piney as she fed her chickens, the cow, and the heifer. Blanche and Charlie were still married but they hadn't lived together for years. He continued to supply her and Piney with coal and wood as well as hay and corn for the animals. If a fence on Piney's property needed to be mended or an animal needed to be bought, sold, doctored, or butchered, he was the one who did it. I couldn't let myself think he wouldn't return.

With much to do and most of us working, we were always shuffling duties. After Hettie joined her brother and Otis at the university, Wanda Rose had assumed the burden of being the only young person left at home, a change she seemed to regard as a privilege. We may have depended on her too much. That evening when Wanda and I left Piney's house, Wanda Rose was busy in the kitchen, rolling out biscuit dough and stewing a quart of tomatoes for their supper.

Freddy had taken the Ford so he could help his father close the store and drive him home, so I rode with Wanda. She was energized by the successful delivery of the calf, but worried about Blanche and Piney.

"I gotta be at the hospital tomorrow, so someone will have to go and help Piney if Blanche is no better," Wanda said.

"Hettie and I will take turns looking in on them. And Wanda Rose. That girl's a wonder."

"Ain't she just? And her such a stinker when she was little," Wanda said. "Who would've thought?"

"I'm not at all surprised," I said, "because I remember *you*. And her father. And Charlie."

"Yeah, all stinkers. Otis too, and look at him now, tall and serious." Wanda smiled sadly. Then she said, "The farm boys got here just in time, didn't they? I'm happy to see all our kids so grown and good looking and all still friends. Otis wants to help at the hospital while he's here—that'll be good for his training and good for the hospital 'cause we always need extra hands. And it looks like Jonah Jr. and Hettie hasn't changed their feelings."

"Hettie doesn't tell me anything, but they do seem serious," I said.

"She couldn't hardly marry into a better family," Wanda said.

I shook my head. "Not soon, I hope. They're young."

"Sure. And we want them to finish school. But they're older than we were."

"Thank goodness for that." A young, untested romance was always interesting, though sometimes it produced anxiety in those of us who knew too well how love could go wrong.

The headlights of Wanda's car did not do much to brighten the half mile between the road to Piney's and the turn to our lane. There were no streetlights or houses along this stretch, just the river on one side and a wooded hill on the other. When we were close to our turn, we saw lights at Glory's shop.

"Glory's got her crew working late," Wanda said.

"Likely it's just her."

"And Virgie."

"Her, too."

Wanda laughed. "Arguing about something, you bet'cha."

Most likely Wanda's assessment was correct. "I don't know why they keep bringing their disagreements to me! Virgie wants Glory to expand Glory Wear with a line of expensive women's dresses. She agrees they'd sell fewer items but claims the profit would be greater."

"Let me guess: Glory wants to go on as they are, making more so they can sell for less," Wanda said.

"She says they must be competitive. Virgie is frustrated because she says their current product wastes the talent of their seamstresses. And I suppose she means her own talent as a designer, too. I wish they wouldn't try to involve me—I know nothing about business. As far as I know, they both could be right."

Glory and Virgie had been collaborating and arguing about clothing design for years, starting in the small shop in Richmond where they'd made one-of-a-kind dresses for wealthy women.

"Here's what I think," Wanda said. "They come to you

because you listen and you don't tell them to leave you outa their problems, like I would."

I sighed. "Barlow says they're two sides of the same coin. He's the businessman in the family—I wish they'd discuss these things with him. Every time Virgie gets one of her ideas Glory says Virgie should start her own shop. Virgie says she can't do that because she doesn't want to give up her movie theater."

Wanda turned the coupe into our lane, and we saw the lights of home. "So when they complain to you, what do you say?"

"I've told them again and again to consider the other's point of view. It's such an old argument. Virgie says she needs to keep Glory on her toes, but I suspect she thinks she's smarter about this business. I suppose she also thinks she's a better designer. And she's older, so she probably thinks she's wiser too."

"It don't hurt to have someone challenge how we do stuff," Wanda said. "You know I never liked anybody telling me what to do, but Will said I had to listen if I wanted to get better. I'm just glad I never had to learn from Virgie."

"Even if she is your oldest and dearest friend."

"So she thinks."

"So she *is*. Barlow says a business has no choice; if it doesn't move forward, it will slip backward. I know Glory and Virgie want to change with the times. The trouble is, what are these times? How can anyone know the choices to make and the best direction to go? What's coming next?"

"Ha. War is coming next, that's what."

War. It seemed far away but just around the corner.

"Barlow has stopped talking about it, so I know he's worried we'll get involved in what's going on overseas, like the last time."

Wanda stopped the car in front of the house. "I can't worry about what's next; I got my hands full with today. Shoot, I still have my hands full with whatever I was supposed to do *yesterday.* So remind me, what are we doing this week?"

"There'll be just us, Christmas Eve, and just us for Christmas dinner," I said. "Hettie is disappointed that we're not hosting the New Year's Eve party, but I haven't the energy for it, and Barlow will need a week to recover from Christmas shoppers. Glory is giving a New Year's party for her employees, and we're all invited."

"Barlow should sell that store," Wanda said.

I agreed. "I've suggested he sell or get someone to manage it, but he likes having his head full of business. I don't know what he'd do without it."

Wanda turned off the motor and we sat in the car for a moment, listening to the stillness and looking up at the starry sky. Then she said, "We better make the most of this Christmas. Someday the kids might not come home even for the holidays. They'll be like my Evie, with their own lives and homes far away." She sniffed. "What will Christmas be with none of my kids?"

"It will be whatever we make it," I said. Arm in arm, we went into the house, greeted by warmer air, the aroma of fresh coffee, and the sound of youthful voices in the kitchen.

We found Hettie and Otis at the kitchen table with Dessie, drinking coffee.

"They needed a little pick-me-up," Dessie said.

I lifted the cookie jar from the pantry and set it on the table. The few cookies in the jar were Fig Newtons, purchased weeks ago and now hard as rocks. "These will soften up if you dunk them in your coffee. Dessie, have they told you about the calf?"

"Oh, my, did they just. More'n I ever wanted to know." She nodded toward the work table. "May Rose, I got them chickens cut up and the potatoes is ready to go on the stove."

"Wonderful," I said, easing myself into a chair.

Wanda washed her hands at the sink, put on a clean apron, and dredged a chicken leg in flour.

Hettie got up and poured my coffee. "So we are allowed to have cookies now? Otis, I suppose this means we're truly grown up—we may have sweets before supper."

"It's only 'cause you been away so long," Dessie said. "We have to spoil you, so you'll keep coming home."

Wanda set two iron skillets to heat on the stovetop. "Do you figure Charlie's got home yet?"

"If you want, I'll drive over there and see," Otis said. "Is there something I should tell him?"

I took my first sip of coffee, relaxing as its warmth expanded my throat. "You may tell him about the calf and say we're hoping he'll be with us Christmas day. Tell him dinner will be at four. Oh, yes. Blanche is sick. Tell him that."

CHAPTER 4

Freddy and Barlow got home from the store just as Otis was hanging his jacket on a hall peg. Barlow shook hands with Otis and hugged Hettie, who came from the kitchen to greet him. I stood back, eager to hear if Otis had found Charlie but distracted by the view of my husband and son together, Freddy the taller, but looking so much like Barlow. Freddy also was a quiet, private sort, a trait I'd come to appreciate. My husband seldom shared his feelings with anyone but me, and I suspected he didn't tell me everything. I hoped my son confided in someone.

In contrast, Otis seemed to be heedless of what he said or who might be listening. I'd had many occasions to observe the boys with a group of friends, Freddy the observer and Otis the life of the party. Unless Wanda Rose was there. She might be the baby among them, but her lively manner dominated every gathering. Little stinkers, Wanda had called them. In both I saw their mother's courage and their father's stubborn dedication.

As usual, I assessed my husband for signs of fatigue. Barlow never complained, but he walked more slowly and sat and stood with more effort and care, and at times his appetite was poor. His hair was still thick and black, but his cheeks were less full, and he was slightly stooped. People not acquainted with us often assumed we were the grandparents of our children, not their parents. At times, to our embarrassment, they thought Barlow was my father. He was older by 16 years.

"Uncle Charlie's house is dark and cold," Otis reported.

I thanked him for checking. "I'm sure everything is fine." Barlow's careful nod said he recognized the uncertainty in my voice. We all seemed falsely cheerful, all anxious about the one who'd been gone too long.

"Dinner smells great," Freddy said.

"And it's ready. Come to the table."

We separated, the men to wash and Hettie and I to help Wanda carry in two heaping platters of fried chicken, mashed potatoes, and a bowl of our home-canned green beans.

Having so many of us reunited at our table helped me set aside my worries. Tom helped Dessie to her chair, and Freddy and Otis stood to shake Tom's hand. Tom had been with us so long he was like a favorite brother and uncle. The children loved his stories of the logging camp, and I was grateful for his good spirit and his constant consideration for his wife. We all tried to relieve Dessie of work, though she often couldn't be stopped unless Tom lifted her out of the way, or she agreed her legs could not carry her one more step.

Our young people were visibly happy to be with us, and we were all curious about events in their lives, which had become more mysterious than ever. I reminded myself that I probably hadn't known everything about my children since they were five, the last time they were fully in my care. Today they had the mystique of beloved strangers, having familiar faces and voices but too many experiences beyond our knowing.

Hettie seemed to have changed the most. She had more confidence about her, like she knew she was not the same as everyone else, but certainly their equal. At her age, I'd been so timid.

Our dinner conversation buzzed with inquiries about Blanche and Piney and stories about the young people's activities at school, but I could tell Wanda was working hard to be merry. I felt an edge of anger. Charlie was always doing this to us, going away with no notice.

After we'd finished the main course and were passing dessert bowls of tapioca pudding, Barlow said, "How were your exams?"

Otis shrugged.

"Not bad," Freddy said. "About what I expected."

"Horrible," Hettie answered.

Freddy shook his head. "She always worries, then she comes out on top."

"It's painful. I should never have enrolled in the business college," she said. "Economics is interesting: so many new ideas, but I don't understand most of it. It's the same with philosophy. There's too much to read and I'm always behind."

"Yet your grades are always better than ours," Freddy said.

"I don't know why that is, when I feel so ignorant."

"We all feel stupid," Otis said. "I'm sure that's what higher education is for—so you'll discover how much there is to know and how little you'll ever understand." He smiled for everyone at the table. "Hettie is simply less ignorant than the rest of us."

Tom laughed. "I don't need to go away and spend a lot of money to learn I'm ignorant."

"Oh, it's all important. You could say we're getting a foundation," Otis said. "Nobody can know everything, but a good foundation opens up new directions, and we follow some of those to learn more and more." He directed his smile to his mother. "Like medical school."

"Well put," Barlow said. "So, Hettie, do you see new directions?"

"Yeah, straight to the altar," Freddy said.

At this, Hettie's face turned pink. "I'd love to have a home and family someday, but not for a long time." She turned to me. "Mom, it's wonderful to be here at last. All so familiar and cozy and safe."

Barlow's eyebrows shot up. "Do you not feel safe at school?"

"Oh, yes, I feel safe. I only mean it's not the same, living among strangers. It's perfectly safe." She smiled at her father. "Very safe. If we go out at night we must sign in and out of the dormitory, so the housemother knows where we are, and we must be in by ten o'clock. That's for women; men don't have hours. I'm not sure that's fair."

I couldn't imagine where anyone needed to be after ten at night.

"No doubt the hours have been established to protect you," Barlow smiled. "And to reassure worried fathers."

"Actually, the university is less dangerous than most places," Otis said. Think of the dangerous territory and risky places here, like the kinds of places Uncle Charlie goes."

With the mention of Charlie's name, our pretense dissolved.

"Your Uncle Charlie has a heavy duty," Barlow said. "We're grateful for lawmen like him."

I had to agree, though from the day the sheriff had sworn him in as a deputy, I'd wished the duty of upholding the law had fallen to someone else.

Hettie said, "So nobody has seen or heard of him for what, two days?"

"You know Charlie," Tom said. "He'll show up."

Otis scraped a last bit of pudding from his dessert dish. "If he's not back by tomorrow, we'll go looking for him."

"No, we won't," Wanda said, her tone grim. "If he's not back tomorrow, we'll call the sheriff."

Leaning heavily on the arms of his chair, Barlow rose with a pronouncement. "And now us old folks will have a rest in the parlor while you young ones clear the table and wash the dishes. Does that sound about right, May Rose?"

"I'll join you soon," I said. Wanda and I followed our children to the kitchen, not because we didn't trust their work, but to be near them as long as we could.

CHAPTER 5

Otis stepped up to be our dishwasher, and his swift, careful handling of the implements reminded me of his father. He also had a sharp chin like Will and all the Herffs, but his hair was rusty-brown and curly, like Wanda's, and he had her light brown eyes and thick lashes. He'd already been accepted to medical school.

There were too many of us crowded around the kitchen sink, washing, drying, and putting away the glassware, dishes, cutlery, and pots and pans, but I enjoyed the young people too much to suggest any one of us wasn't needed. Their chatter hinted of the lives they lived apart from us.

When I could watch them unnoticed, I searched the faces of my loved ones and listened to their voices for signs of happiness or trouble. I sensed they told me only the best of their lives. Hettie's confession about her lack of comprehension, however, was an old story. She'd never felt as knowledgeable as others, though she'd always been a good student. I profoundly wished a life of peace and happiness for her and Freddy, and for Wanda's children too. If their future turned out to be hard, I prayed that love and strong friendships would be their compensation.

Hettie asked casually if the Watsons would be coming for our New Year's party this year.

"I'm sorry, didn't I tell you? Your father and I decided not to have the party this year."

"But it's a tradition," Freddy said. "Does everyone know? I can see half the town showing up and all of us in bed."

"I think everyone knows," Wanda said. "Your ma started telling them at last year's party. This year Glory is having a New Year's Eve thing at the shop. It's for her workers and their families, but we're invited too."

Otis winked at me. "Hettie doesn't care where the party is as long as the Watsons are there. Or one of them."

The others laughed. Hettie was saved by the ringing of the phone. We paused, listening for the three short rings of the party line that meant a caller wanted someone in this house.

"I'll get it," Hettie said.

Her brother smiled. "She's hoping it's him. And she saw him how many hours ago?"

"Freddy," Wanda said, "how about you? do you have a girl-friend? Somebody here, somebody there?"

He smiled and shrugged.

So there was someone? Obviously, he was not going to talk about it. Like his father, Freddy was a private person.

Hettie came back to the kitchen, her voice urgent. "It's Wanda Rose. She wants her mom."

Wanda was gone only a few seconds, returning with her coat over her arm. "Don't know when I'll be back. Wanda Rose is scared, she says Blanche is hollering mean things about Piney, and poor Piney can't stop crying."

Otis stepped away from the sink and motioned Freddy to take his place. "Mom, wait while I get my coat."

When they left, Freddy rolled up his sleeves and set a skillet into the dishwater. "Maybe I shouldn't say this, but hasn't Blanche always been odd?"

"Sometimes people talk out of their heads when they're fevered," I said. "Truly, Blanche has been very dependable since Piney... you know, since Piney hasn't been herself."

"They're lucky to have Wanda," Hettie said.

So many were lucky to have her. Twice heartbroken by the deaths of two good husbands, she filled her life by meeting the needs of her family and the hospital. I wished someone wanted to make her happy. Another husband, I meant. Wanda insisted there was no room in her heart for another man. I understood that, too.

Hettie wanted to know if we'd have company for Christmas dinner.

"We expect Blanche and Piney," I said, "but Glory is cooking for Randolph and Johnny this year."

"Wow. Glory is cooking," Hettie said. "That's as unexpected as Father taking over the kitchen. What next?"

"Charlie. He said he'd join us for Christmas dinner, so he'll be here." It was my Christmas wish.

~

THE TELEPHONE RANG SEVERAL TIMES AFTER WANDA AND OTIS left, but the rings were for other customers on our party line.

On any other night, I'd have retired with a newspaper to the sitting room in our apartment and exchanged my tight shoes and stockings for my comfortable, worn-out house shoes, but hours with my children had become so rare that I didn't want to miss a moment. I sat with them in the parlor, listening to the Glen Miller orchestra on the radio, looking at the ads in an old copy of *The Pittsburg Press*, and wondering how Wanda was getting along with Blanche and Piney.

Everyone had a portion of a newspaper, from time to time exchanging pages or picking up an older issue from the stack on the table in front of the window. I looked at the pictures and prices in ads for clothing and hats and the many suggestions for Christmas gifts, though mine were already bought.

Dessie murmured about the doings of rich people featured in the society pages. Barlow read state, national and world news, but he'd stopped sharing his thoughts about world happenings after Japan's invasion of China and the atrocities of the Nazis in Germany. He'd become profoundly silent on these subjects, as though no words were adequate to express his outrage. Also, he knew my feelings. None of our family or friends had been drafted to fight in Europe in the last war, but all our young people were of fighting age now. I did not want to send any of them to war.

"Mom," Freddy said. "Have you cut a tree yet? We could set it up."

"I was hoping you'd go out and find one tomorrow," I said. For the past week I'd thought about asking Charlie or Tom to cut a small pine and set it up in the parlor where I could decorate it little by little. Had I done that, our young people would have come home to the scent of pine and a vision of color and cheer. I wished I'd done more than think about it. Without festive decoration, our parlor was dark and drab, everything faded and worn.

Barlow folded his paper and stood with a slight stretch of his back, straightening his shoulders and twisting the kinks out of his neck. "I'm afraid I must say goodnight. If you youngsters don't have other plans, I could use help in the store tomorrow. It will be a busy day."

"I plan to be there," Hettie said.

"Me too," Freddy said. "I can cut a tree soon as it's light, before the store opens. Then we can decorate it tomorrow night."

"We must have warm spiced cider," Hettie said. "Do we have cider?"

"I believe we do."

"Dessie, I'm going to bed," Tom said. "You coming?"

"I'll sit a while longer," she said.

"Goodnight, then." He made his way to the bedroom on the other side of the entryway, the one created from the former boardinghouse office plus the nursery on the other side of our apartment. Our house suited us well, even if it had seen better days.

"Goodnight all," Barlow said, turning to leave. "It's good to have all of you home again."

"Sure is," Dessie said.

Freddy turned down the radio volume, which had been set high so Tom could hear.

It had been a strange homecoming for the young people, with Blanche sick and Piney confused and the episode of the struggling heifer and her calf, but for me, being together made every difficulty easier and every outcome easier to manage.

How hard it would be, I often think, to bear our troubles alone.

"Otis and Wanda has been gone quite a while," Dessie said.

At that moment, the phone rang. Hettie sat until she was sure of the three short rings, then hurried to answer it. After she said hello, I pretended to study my paper while listening for a sound of pleasure that might mean Jonah Jr. was on the other end of the line. The few words she uttered sounded urgent.

"That was Otis," she said, hurrying back. "He wants someone to pick up Wanda Rose and Piney and bring them here for the night. He and Wanda are taking Blanche to the hospital."

"I'll drive over and get them," Freddy said.

"I should go," I said. We never knew who Piney might remember or how she'd react to the simplest change.

"Together, then." Freddy took my long winter coat from the hall peg and held it while I slipped my arms into the sleeves.

He left to warm up the car, and I stepped back into the parlor for advice. "If we're to keep Piney for the night, where's the best place for her to sleep?"

"Put her close to you or Wanda," Dessie said. "If Piney wakes, likely she won't know where she is."

"Wanda may stay at the hospital with Blanche," I said.

Hettie asked, "Do you still have a daybed in the playroom?"

"We do. I believe it's the best choice." The old playroom was the small room at the other end of the apartment. I could leave its door open and hear Piney if she called out. I could also lock the apartment door in case she felt inclined to wander in the night.

"I'll find sheets for the daybed," Hettie said.

Dessie said she'd stay up awhile in case I needed help when we returned with Piney.

Freddy drove carefully, swerving to avoid the potholes that showed in the car's headlights. On Piney's road, lights glowed from houses on the right, but the left side was mostly in darkness. A single light marked Piney's house.

"Oh, May Rose," Piney said, when Freddy and I entered her kitchen. "Blanche is sick."

Piney sat at the scarred wooden table and Wanda Rose stood by, her face anxious. They were already wearing their coats, and Piney had a tapestry-covered valise clutched in her hand.

"I know, dear. The hospital will make her better. We've come to take you to our house so we can be together. Won't that be nice?"

I took Piney's arm and helped her stand. Wanda Rose took the valise and Freddy opened the door. "We're going to get a Christmas tree tomorrow," he said.

Piney smiled. "I love a Christmas tree. Will everyone be there?"

I said yes, though I was afraid she meant her late husband and his grandchildren, since she often talked about them as though they'd just stepped out for a few minutes.

"Everyone who can make it will be there," Freddy said. "We're hoping to see Charlie, too."

"But Blanche is sick," she said.

"I know." I put my arm through Piney's and gave it a squeeze. "Wanda will take care of her."

CHAPTER 6

That night I slept with one ear alert, my method when my little ones were sick, though this time I listened for Piney. I heard only soft snoring from the playroom, but I jarred awake when I heard the click of our front door, then slow steps up the stairs. Wanda's slow, tired steps. I wanted to ask about Blanche, but did not want to keep her awake with talk.

The clock in the hall struck two, and an upstairs door closed softly.

Beside me, Barlow lay in deep sleep. All seemed well, but where was Charlie sleeping this night? "I'm okay, Ma," he'd said so many times in his youth. "You got to stop worrying about me." Sometimes I thought my tendency to worry had made him secretive, yet hadn't he been that way as a child in his father's home? In those days, there'd been nobody to worry about him. In those days, Wanda had called him "sneaky."

The chimes of the clock in the hall were soft and mellow, and so familiar that usually they passed without notice, but I heard the clock chime again at five.

I didn't have to rush off to work because the school where I taught fourth grade was closed for the holidays. I'd been thinking: if Barlow wouldn't give up the store, I should quit my job and work there with him. I didn't have the proper education for teaching, and every summer I thought the school might find someone more qualified. But I'd been there for almost ten years, hired each September "on an emergency basis."

This morning I needed to cook breakfast for a lot of people and prepare sack lunches for the ones going out to work. Then there'd be advance preparations for our evening meal and for tomorrow, Christmas day. I still needed to wrap Christmas gifts, and I should clean the dining room chandelier. And I'd almost forgotten—watch over Piney. I needed to see about her first.

I dressed quietly and softly closed our bedroom door, then peered into the playroom. Piney slept on, like a Christmas blessing.

The house was unusually warm for a December morning, but I did not want the furnace fire to go out even if we didn't need it. I opened the draft and went to the basement and shoveled a few lumps of coal onto the embers.

When I returned to the kitchen, Dessie was scooping coffee into the percolator. "I been awake for hours," she said. "Did Piney give you any trouble?"

"She slept peacefully, but you'll need a nap today."

"I nap most days," she said. "Sometimes one in the morning and one in the afternoon."

"Good," I said. "Maybe I'll nap too." I was already wound too tight for sleep.

"Hot in here," Dessie said.

We had a new electric stove, but on cold winter mornings we built a fire in the old woodstove. Not today. Dessie opened the back door a crack to cool us down.

Wanda came drowsily into the kitchen before six, dressed in her flannel robe and old slippers, her hair wild and unbrushed.

Dessie was at the kitchen table with her coffee, and I was sipping mine standing up. I had two iron skillets heating on the electric stove.

Dessie said, "Well? How's Blanche?"

"She was breathing better when I left. Doc Madison said she has pneumonia. He gave her that sulfa medicine. Otis stayed because the hospital is short an orderly. He said he'd call if she gets worse."

"So no news is good news," I said, something I needed to keep in mind. "Piney's still sleeping. She's not been a bit of trouble."

"Good. Did she call out for Blanche?"

"Only once, early last evening. I told her Blanche was sick and she said yes, she knew. Do you have to go to work early? I don't think you got much sleep."

"I slept a couple of hours." She poured her coffee and carried the cup to the table. Then she slumped into a chair across from Dessie. "Maybe one of the kids can drive me to work. I'll send Otis home to sleep. Get someone to pick me up at the end of the day; I know I won't feel up to walking. I guess this is Christmas Eve?"

"It is. Everybody will be down soon. Freddy's going to cut a tree, and we'll decorate it tonight. Today he and Hettie are going to help Barlow in the store." I spooned bacon grease into the skillet and watched it melt.

"I'm sorry to stick you with an extra burden," Wanda said. "Get Wanda Rose to watch over Piney or help with whatever you need."

"We'll get along okay. Wanda Rose has already done so much. Maybe she'll have plans with her friends. She should have some fun."

"Maybe, but don't you know she's always trying to outdo the older kids. She kept on visiting Piney even though she knew Blanche didn't like her and didn't want her there. I think Blanche was jealous because Wanda Rose was always Piney's favorite. Anyway, Blanche has changed. These days she's glad Wanda Rose comes around and stays with Piney from time to time so she can get out and shop and such."

"Wanda Rose is such an adult," I said. "And soon the age difference between her and our older ones will be nothing. Just look at us."

Wanda squinted and her mouth turned down. "Are you saying I'm as old as you and Dessie?"

I shrugged. "Being as you're so bossy, I consider you my elder."

"Your *what?*"

"My *beautiful* elder."

"Your beautiful elder *daughter*," Wanda said.

Dessie laughed. "Girls, we're still kids, full of fairy stories and crazy waiting for Santy Claus."

Both skillets were sizzling with dried beef, and we were laughing when Freddy came into the kitchen wearing old clothes and boots and carrying a jacket. "Are you ladies telling stories? Anything fit for a kid's ears?"

He sounded so sensible and grown up. I wanted him to have fun this holiday, too.

"We're addled, that's all," Dessie said. "And it's Christmas."

Wanda pushed herself up from the table. "A laugh's as easy as a moan. But now I gotta get presentable for work." She left by the back stairway.

Freddy hung the jacket over a chair. "May I possibly eat early? I want to get that tree soon as it's light."

"Breakfast will be ready in a minute," I said, admiring his handsome profile, his clear eyes and unassuming manner. I'd heard his friends call him *Fred*. The name seemed wrong, but appropriate, I supposed, for life as an adult. My boy, Mr. Fred Townsend.

"Set a place for yourself here, and if you would, please carry the rest of the plates to the dining room."

Abruptly and without explanation he smiled. To me, his smile felt like love. He was glad to be home and happy to be in our old kitchen with Dessie and me.

He set the buffet with plates and flatware in short order, and Dessie began slicing bread for toast. Then he stood nearby with his coffee while I mixed flour into the shreds of beef. The skillet sizzled and steamed. I added water and a bit of cream and stirred the mixture into gravy. He opened the sides of the toaster and set in his slices of bread, and when the toast was ready, he put the slices on a plate and dipped gravy from one of the skillets. I set the skillets on unheated burners, ready to heat again when the others were ready to eat. It was a rare, companionable moment, working in the kitchen with my son, known in his part of the world as *Fred*.

Shortly before daylight, he went out to cut a tree from our hillside but came back right away for his father's old oilcloth coat, saying there was a light rain.

The house was coming awake. Barlow had predicted a time when we'd have no more guests, no one living here but family. Now at times I thought we were too few, but not today. I loved hearing the soft sounds of doors closing, distant conversations, and light treads on the stairs.

Piney slept on, and we sat down to breakfast without her, though she and Blanche were foremost on our minds. Wanda Rose said, "Yesterday Aunt Piney called me Evalena. She said I was her little sister."

"Piney did have a younger sister by that name," I said.

Wanda Rose said, "My grandmother."

"That's right. This was the first time I'd heard either of Wanda's children speak of their grandmother, who'd lived with Jamie Long, their grandfather. We'd let our children assume that Jamie had been married to Evalena before he married me. We knew sadder truths, but Wanda and I had never disclosed those to our children. For sure, Evalena had been an unfortunate woman. Perhaps the young people had heard from other sources.

Wanda continued to eat as though distracted. Dessie smiled sadly, because she knew. She'd been a cook in Hester Townsend's boardinghouse when Evalena worked in the town brothel, long before the old Winkler was destroyed by fire and flood. "I guess I won't mind getting dotty if I'm as sweet as Piney," Dessie said.

Tom pinched her cheek, and she slapped at his hand in irritation, evoking smiles from Hettie and Wanda Rose. "Dessie, you are my one and only sweetheart," he said, "but don'cha know, there's nobody sweeter than Piney."

Wanda looked up from her food. "Whatever happens, I don't want her to be anxious and afraid." Around the table, heads nodded.

Thinking of Piney and listening to the chatter of our young people that morning, I had a sense that great changes were coming to our family. Our young people were excited about their futures, but I couldn't keep away a sense of sadness. There would be an end to precious times like this, changes that would not be so nice. I didn't mind some of the obvious ones, like the dusty chandelier above my head. Keeping the glass crystals shiny no longer seemed important.

We older folks had seen too much, the rough times of the sawmill town, the struggles of cold and lonely winters, tragedies like Evalena's, disasters in the coal mines, and important people dying too soon. Barlow had lost his sister, Hester, and Piney had lost Simpson, her husband, friend and helper to us all. Likewise we'd mourned Wanda's Uncle Russell. And how we missed Will! With each death, we'd wondered how we'd possibly get along without these people. *And now.* I couldn't let myself think that Charlie was gone too.

This was the morning of Christmas Eve, and the family was almost all together, with Freddy's cut pine waiting on the porch.

For the sake of my family, I needed to be cheerful. Whatever was ahead for our young people, I wanted them to be happy too, with love and purpose and friendships to sustain them. I wanted them to have children, life's greatest blessing.

That's what Christmas was about, the birth of a child.

CHAPTER 7

When we heard steps on the porch, I was mixing pie dough, and Wanda Rose was putting away breakfast dishes. Dessie sat at the table, peeling apples, and Otis and Piney were eating the remains of the dried beef on toast. Because everyone else was at work and only family used the back door, I thought, *Charlie, at last*! I looked up, scraping flour from my fingers as the door opened with a cautious squeak.

At the table, Otis set down his fork. "Aunt Glory! Good morning!" He stood and gave her a quick kiss on the cheek.

"How wonderful," she said. "A kiss from a handsome young man. Welcome home, Otis." She pulled off leather driving gloves and blew a kiss to Wanda Rose. "Hello, sweetheart, Merry Christmas, everyone. Piney, how nice to see you."

Glory had lovely dark eyes and dark hair like her brothers, beautifully offset this morning by a fitted red coat and matching red tam. She always looked stylish, but not because she was wealthier than the rest of us. Style was largely a matter of confidence, I believed, and Glory would look stylish if she were the poorest. This morning her lovely eyes drooped, and I wondered if she'd worked all night.

Piney reached one hand toward Glory and braced the other on the tabletop, trying to stand.

"No need to get up, dear, no need," Glory said. "Sit right there and enjoy your breakfast."

Piney dropped to her seat. "You're a pretty lady."

"Thank you. So are you," Glory said.

Otis touched Piney's arm. "Aunt Piney, do you remember Glory?"

Piney nodded. "Very glad to meet you."

"And you." Glory bent and kissed her cheek.

"Glory," I said. "There's a fresh pot of coffee. Will you have some?"

"Just a sip," she said. "With a little milk or cream if you have it." Otis offered his chair and she sat and slipped her coat from her shoulders and propped it over the back of the chair.

When I set her coffee on the table she said, "Well? Is there news?" It was a pointed question, one that assumed I knew what she wanted: information about Charlie.

I didn't know how much she knew, and I wasn't going to share my concerns in Piney's hearing. "Let's see. Freddy and Hettie are helping Barlow in the store today. Blanche is sick, but she'll soon be better, because she's in the hospital. Wanda is at work there now. Piney's heifer has a new bull calf, and Otis worked at the hospital last night."

"My goodness," Glory said. "What a busy family! I'm glad to hear Blanche will soon be well, and I'm happy about your calf, Piney." She drained her coffee in one gulp, then said, "And now, May Rose, shall we share some Christmas secrets?"

"Christmas secrets, how exciting! Give me a moment." I dampened a dish towel and covered the mixture of flour and lard. Then I washed my doughy hands and followed her to the parlor.

She whirled to face me. "So, did Charlie come home?"

"What do you know?"

"Wanda called yesterday and asked if I'd seen Charlie. That's a laugh! Everybody sees him more than I do. I think he forgets he has a sister. My son adores him, but I'm not sure Charlie remembers Johnny's name—he never says it. What does that tell you?"

"I don't know. Does he call any of us by name?" Gradually we'd accepted Charlie's ways. We had to be thankful, considering how damaged he'd been, all those years ago, when Russell brought him home to Winkler. He hadn't seemed to know us, and we weren't certain he knew his own name. He'd been suspicious of everyone.

This year he'd promised to join us for Christmas dinner. I'd reminded him how everything changes, that we seldom saw our grown-up children, and someday they might be far away.

Glory said, "Old John Johnson told Randolph that Charlie was two days late. That was yesterday. Do you know anything more?"

"Nothing more. Otis drove up to his house this morning on his way home from the hospital. The house is cold and there's no sign of Charlie's truck."

"So wherever he went, he took the truck."

"He might have thought the weather would change." Taking the truck was unusual, since Charlie preferred traveling by horseback, especially since so many people in the mountains did not live on proper roads. "Wanda said if he wasn't back by noon today, we should call the sheriff."

"Can you do it now? I'll wait."

"Would you like to make the call?" I always felt inadequate, questioning strangers on the telephone, especially someone official, like the sheriff.

"Gladly," she said. She sat at the telephone desk in the hall and asked the operator to connect her to the county sheriff. I stood nearby, where I could watch her face.

"The operator's ringing the number," Glory said. "Oh, hello? May I please speak to the sheriff?" She listened, frowning, then said, "Do you know where he went?" I watched for a smile of satisfaction and for her anxious eyes to relax but neither of these things happened.

"Thank you," she said. "If you learn something, would you call this number in Winkler? 6242. Or you may call 312. I'm Deputy Herff's sister, Glory Bell. 312 is my number. 6242 is the home of May Rose and Barlow Townsend. Townsend, that's right. We're very eager to learn about Charlie—he was expected to come home days ago. Yes, thank you." She replaced the receiver and looked up. "Well, that's something. That was the sheriff's wife. This morning he and a deputy drove off to check the property where he sent Charlie."

"Good," I said, releasing a suspended breath.

"She said he hasn't returned yet. There was a disturbance at that place, a woman threatening her neighbors with a shotgun. One of the woman's neighbors went down to Jennie Town and phoned the sheriff. But the day the sheriff got the call he had to testify at the courthouse, so he sent Charlie to the mine guard-house at Jennie Town, where the neighbor said he'd leave directions to the trouble. The neighbor who phoned the sheriff was a Barney Temple, and he said the one causing the trouble was an old woman, Jessie somebody. They all live in an abandoned logging camp somewhere near Jennie Town.

Suddenly dizzy, I plopped into the nearest chair. Jennie Town wasn't far away, a distance walkable in half a day, an hour or more by motor vehicle, depending on the weather. Of course the distance from Jennie Town to the logging camp and the difficulty of getting there could be another story, but hearing Charlie might have been close all this time doubled my sense that something was very wrong.

"So today the sheriff will learn something," Glory said.

Right away my thoughts jumped to the worst possible outcome, that the sheriff might arrive to find Charlie shot or his truck wrecked. Why else would he not have come home days ago?

"Don't say anything to the children," I said, imagining Otis and Freddy and even Wanda Rose hurrying away to search for him. "I should have called the sheriff yesterday, when we realized Charlie had been gone too long."

"Charlie should have called so we wouldn't worry. This isn't like the old days, May Rose, when we had no telephones."

"There aren't phones everywhere," I said, though of course she knew that. Our town was lucky to have clever men like her husband and Will Herff, who'd created our telephone system. When Will and Wanda lived in the country, he'd extended the line to their farmhouse to oblige her. Other little towns weren't as fortunate.

"I can't just go on thinking he's all right. Can you?"

"Not now." I'd tried to believe Charlie was safe, merely delayed for good reason. "I feel like I should do something."

"We should go down there," she said. "Go to Jennie Town and find that logging camp. Our Christmas dinners aren't important, are they? We can have Christmas dinner any day."

My thoughts went from certainty that I couldn't possibly abandon today's responsibilities to the certainty that Charlie was in trouble and nothing was as important as finding him. "We're hardly the best people to search," I said. "Especially not if he needs to be rescued."

"Of course we're not the best," she said. "Charlie's the best man for search and rescue, isn't he? Randolph might go with us. Since he used to manage the Jennie Town Mine, he knows the area and some of the people. But not Uncle Barlow. Let's keep him out of it, please."

"I'll have to tell him," I said. "And he won't like us going, not one little bit."

CHAPTER 8

In the kitchen, Dessie and Wanda Rose were trying to console Piney, who was crying and shaking her head in a frantic way. Wanda Rose held her hand.

"Piney, you know me," Dessie said. "We was in school together, remember? You and me and Evalena, your sister. I'm Dessie."

Piney brought Wanda Rose's hand to her cheek. "This is my Evalena. I don't know you."

"Her over there is May Rose. You and her is great friends," Dessie said. "She's Wanda's stepma. You and May Rose go way back. And this is Glory, Charlie's sister."

"Blanche is sick," Piney cried.

"But she's getting better," Wanda Rose said. "I know what we'll do—we'll go to your house. You can brush my hair."

Nodding agreement, Piney patted her wet face with the hem of her apron. Wanda Rose took her arm and led her from the kitchen.

Glory took her coat from the peg. "I'm sorry about this, so much trouble all at once. But I'm going to do what I said. Maybe you should stay here."

"I need to go with you," I said. "I'll call Wanda and make sure it's okay to leave Piney with Wanda Rose. Then I'll see Barlow. If everyone agrees, you can pick me up at the store."

Glory left by the back door, then popped back inside. "It's raining again. Best wear old shoes." She hurried out again.

Dessie watched, perplexed. "What's happening? Where are you going and why do you need old shoes?"

Hurriedly I described what we'd learned from the sheriff's wife and our plans to search for Charlie.

"I don't like it," Dessie said. "You got no idea what you'll find in them hills. This is men's job."

"Randolph will go with us. Everyone else is busy."

"You're busy too. We got dinner to fix for tonight and all that for Christmas day."

"Let's not worry about the pies or what we'll eat tonight," I said. I made two trips to the basement and carried up four quarts of vegetable soup we'd canned last summer. "We'll have soup for supper. Call and ask Barlow to bring home some of those saltines. I'm sure I'll be back before dark, but if we're delayed, we'll telephone."

"You can't call if you have a flat tire between here and Jennie Town."

"So if we're delayed, you'll know it's because we have a flat somewhere between here and there."

"*Oh, you,*" Dessie said. She looked toward the back porch where a hard rain was pounding the tin roof. "Roads is gonna be messy."

PINEY HAD ONCE BEEN AN EXCELLENT PIE-BAKER, SO WANDA Rose decided she and Piney could finish the pies I'd started for Christmas dinner. I didn't know if this was possible, given Piney's condition, but I didn't want to leave the work to Dessie, and

Wanda Rose was eager to try. At the same time, she wanted to go with me to search for Charlie. So did Wanda, who was disappointed because she couldn't leave the hospital.

Now I had to convince my husband. He'd never interfered in my decisions about the boardinghouse, and he hadn't objected when I'd taken the teaching job. This time he might say our plan was unadvised and possibly dangerous. He might, for the first time, say *no*.

It was such a gloomy start, with a gray sky and pouring rain. Best as I could, I held the umbrella over Wanda Rose and Piney as we helped Piney into Wanda's car. Then Wanda Rose and I returned to the porch for the sliced apples and the bowl with the flour and lard for the crusts, which we set on Piney's lap. I held the jar of mincemeat.

Wanda Rose drove, with Piney between us. "We're making pies," Piney said, when I thanked Wanda Rose for taking charge.

During the school year I seldom went to the store, relying on Barlow to bring home what we needed. I always loved seeing him there, finally in a job that made him eager to get up in the morning. Hoping to speak privately, I hurried out of the rain and into the warmth and brightness of the store.

Barlow stood behind the back counter, deftly wrapping string around a brown paper package. His face lifted in a smile when he saw me, causing his customer to turn to look. She was Cilla Jones, an old friend, also a manager at Glory Wear.

"May Rose," she said, when I joined her at the counter. "Merry Christmas! Will we see you at the New Year's party?"

"Merry Christmas, Cilla. We'll be there—we're looking forward to it. Are you expecting Franklin and his family for the holidays?" Cilla was a widow whose son, Franklin, lived in Washington, D.C.

Her eyes sparkled. "They're here now, Franklin and his wife and my grandchildren, Louis and Maurice. He's closed his office for the holidays, so you'll see them at the party."

"Wonderful," I said. This was something we mothers of

grown-up children shared: the delight of having them under our roof again, if only for a few days. Cilla was justly proud of Franklin's achievements, and so were we, but he was her only child, and I knew she wished he did not live so far away. He was a lawyer, one of only a few men of his race to graduate from Harvard Law School.

Barlow set Cilla's packages in her shopping basket, and we promised to talk further at Glory's party. Then she hurried away.

"My dear," Barlow said, turning to me with pleasure, "is there something you need, or did you possibly come to help?"

I took a deep breath, wishing I could say I'd come to help, or I'd only come for a glimpse of him, because in busy times we never seemed to have enough time together. "I need to tell you something. It will take just a minute." The store was crowded as on no other day, shoppers browsing the special displays of candy, dolls, puzzles, toy trucks, Christmas wrapping paper and tree ornaments while they waited to be served.

I could see he wondered why I'd appeared in person, rather than telephoning. "It's about Charlie," I said.

He straightened, as though preparing for something he didn't want to hear. My husband knew me well, and as much as any of us, he knew Charlie.

I went behind the counter and stood close, bending my head and speaking quietly. "We've learned he was sent to settle a disturbance near Jennie Town. Since he could have easily been home days ago, we think he might have met with an accident. He could be lying off some mountain road in his wrecked truck, with no one to find him." I didn't say he might have been shot, but I thought it, and immediately a tear spilled from one eye. I sniffed and swiped my hand over my cheek. If I let my imagination loose, I'd fall apart.

"So Glory and I are going to drive to Jennie Town," I said. "To see the place where he went and learn why he didn't come home.

He left days ago, Barlow. He was supposed to return the same day."

Barlow frowned. "Perhaps the sheriff sent him farther on to some other trouble?"

"We know he didn't," I said. "We called the sheriff this morning and spoke to his wife. The sheriff must be concerned, too, because he and his deputy set off early today to the area where he sent Charlie."

"Then they'll take care of everything. If Charlie's there, they'll send him home."

"*If he's there.* Glory and I feel so useless. Charlie could be so close. We should have done something yesterday. I feel terrible about it."

"First, you're not useless, you're both busy women," Barlow said. "Second, wouldn't you be going on a wild-goose chase? Do you have any idea where to look?"

"Not exactly," I said. "But we'd be three more sets of eyes to look for him. Glory said Randolph will go with us."

"Did she talk you into this?"

"No, no, we decided at the same time. It feels wrong not to try something."

Barlow gazed around the store like he was searching for the words to change my mind. Motioning me to follow, he opened the door to the storage room, an addition at the back of the building with free-standing shelves, currently almost bare of merchandise. I was half-expecting a lecture, but he put his hand on my cheeks and gave me a strong kiss.

"I don't want you going into danger," he whispered.

I wrapped my arms around his waist and lay my cheek against his. "We'll be careful."

"I don't want you to go."

I nodded. "I'm shirking my duties. I know."

"I'd rather go myself," he said. "I don't want you driving into the hills to face something like this without proper help."

"You can't leave the store," I said.

"I could, but I shouldn't, and I wouldn't be much help in a search. Freddy would be better. Take Freddy."

His offer surprised me. "Can you spare him?"

"I'll breathe easier and do my work better knowing he's with you."

"We'll be all right. I promise not to do anything foolish."

"I trust you. Don't let Glory lead you astray."

"She's a responsible person, Barlow."

"She's headstrong."

"She has to be. She's a boss, and she's a woman."

He kissed me again, then turned me toward the door. "I'll have a word with Freddy. Send him back here to me."

CHAPTER 9

Freddy jogged happily out of the store, carrying his sack lunch and a bag of peanuts roasted in their shells. He made no secret of being glad to exchange a demanding day in the store for a ride into the unknown. I think we were heartened by his vigor and optimism.

Randolph drove, with Freddy beside him in the front seat. The two of them talked all the way to Jennie Town, comparing their university experiences, Randolph's work as manager of our electric plant, and Freddy's desire to pilot an airplane, an ambition I was hearing for the first time. Thinking of possible misadventures thousands of feet in the air gave me something new to worry about. I understood why children did not tell their mothers everything.

The road to Jennie Town was paved, but typically roads in the mountains were not, so I was glad when the rain stopped. The sky, however, remained dull and gray. Glory and I stared ahead and did not talk.

Our first stop was the Jennie Mine guardhouse. Before settling in Winkler, Randolph had managed this mine, and he still knew a few people, including the man on guard duty. While they spoke, we waited in the car with our windows rolled down, eager to hear.

"All right," Randolph said, when he returned to the car. "The place is called 'Beauty' and the guard told me how to get there. He's the same one who gave directions to Charlie, and this morning to the sheriff."

Freddie said, "Beauty? I've never heard of it."

"It's an old logging camp," Randolph said. "Not really a town. The guard said it's just a few old shacks of squatters."

The road to Beauty was the first right turn after we passed the last house of Jennie Town. Randolph shifted to a low gear and followed the tracks of vehicles that had gone before us up a steep, rutted road with sharp turns. We bumped slowly along, Randolph swerving to avoid rocks and ruts while the rest of us looked side to side for signs of a wreck, such as tire tracks veering off the side of the hill. Small streams rushed down creases in the hillside, and the ruts as well as ditches along the roadside were full of brown water.

In places, little streams flowed across the road, and seeing tracks of other vehicles that had driven through them, Randolph did too. Then we came to a place where the road was clearly washed out. Not much water flowed through the wide recess of rock and mud cutting off the road, but it looked too deep for Randolph's car to pass through.

Tracks showed that other vehicles had parked at the roadside, but none were there now.

"Here's where we walk," Glory said, opening the door on her side.

"Maybe Freddy and I should scout up the road a ways," Randolph said. "We have no idea how far we might need to go to reach that place, and no idea what we'll find when we get there. We don't want to walk into the middle of a feud."

"I think I smell coffee," I said. "So we couldn't be far from somebody."

Glory pointed to tire tracks in the washed-out portion of the road. "Somebody went through here, possibly not long ago, since the tracks haven't washed away."

"Our car won't go through," Randolph said. "Not without getting hung up on those rocks."

"Which is why I'm walking," Glory said. Prodding the end of her umbrella into the mud, she stepped into the washout. I followed, using the point of my umbrella in the same way. Behind us, I heard the snapping of wood, which turned out to be Randolph and Freddy breaking walking sticks from a downed limb at the roadside.

My shoes got muddy and wet in the washout, and though they had stout soles they were not much protection from the stony road. We trudged on without complaint. I didn't know how many miles I could walk uphill, but fortunately we saw the first small dwellings of the logging camp not long after we rounded the first bend.

The camp named Beauty was no beauty, but I'd seen logging camps before and this one matched my expectations. Two dozen or so houses were built on both sides of a narrow valley called a "holler". The houses looked like the kind built for temporary habitation, possibly of two rooms, all of rough lumber with stove pipe chimneys sticking through drooping roofs covered with tar paper. There was a rough footbridge across the ravine, but no walkways and no electric or telephone lines. Likely the inhabitants carried water from a spring. I also saw sheds and privies, some in ruins.

Many of these dwellings looked to be uninhabited, their windows broken and roofs collapsed, but smoke came from the stovepipes of a few. A man came out of one of these as we approached. He had a shaggy, graying beard, wore sagging bib overalls and a brown cloth hat with the brim turned down.

We waited as Randolph walked closer, looking official in his usual work attire: gray gabardine slacks and shirt and new-looking lace-up boots with speed hooks. "We're looking for Mr. Temple," Randolph said.

The man shook his head in wonder. "You got him. Busy times up here. You're the third to ask."

"And the first?"

"A deputy, t'other day, and awhile ago, the sheriff."

Randolph looked toward the ravine. "Are they here some-where now?"

"The deputy left out about daybreak. The sheriff went soon's he learned what he come for."

Glory stepped forward. "What did the sheriff learn?"

Mr. Temple gave the four of us a suspicious look. "Just who is you folks and what's your business here?"

"I'm the deputy's sister," Glory said. "We're from Winkler, right up the road a few miles."

"I used to work for the Jennie Town mine," Randolph said.

This bit of familiarity seemed to lessen Mr. Temple's uncer-tainty. "All right then. The sheriff found out the standoff was over and done and his deputy was gone. That deputy got into a fine mess, he did."

A standoff. I spoke for the first time. "What kind of mess?"

Mr. Temple nodded. "Well, it's embarrassing to say, because it happened to one of our own. We're a good bunch here, just a few old fellers. We look after each other best we can."

"That's very commendable," Randolph said.

Mr. Temple looked us over. "It's kindly of you folks to come looking for your deputy. He treated old Jessie kindly, too, better'n most would to a woman waving a shotgun."

"Oh, dear," I mumbled.

Mr. Temple yawned. "Pardon me, ma'am. I don't want you all to get the wrong idea about Jessie, for she's had a hard time of it and what she done wasn't natural for her. You gotta understand she got so she didn't know straight up. We only called for the law 'cause she was dangerin' her grandkids and we couldn't handle her our own selves."

Glory reached for my hand, and Freddy squeezed his arm around my shoulders. *Charlie had been in a standoff, but he'd left that day. There were children. Had anyone been shot?*

Freddy spoke up. "Was anyone hurt?"

"When the deputy left, his side was bleeding a little where it caught some pellets, but he said it was just a scratch. Mostly he was worn out, standing behind his truck and talking nice to her all that time while she sat in her doorway with that gun, saying she was gonna shoot us or herself if we took another step. All the while him talking on and on about Christmas, the songs him and her could sing together, gifts they'd go get for the kids, and how he loved pumpkin pie. I heard him sing a snatch of "Jingle Bells." He didn't sing too good, but some of the old fellers here joined in, trying to settle Jessie, you know. I heard him invite her to his house for chicken dinner. Last night I thought he'd about got her to set aside that gun. But she was far gone, outa her mind, like." He pointed to a house across the ravine. "Over there's where it happened. I want to tell you, none of us has slept. I kinda feel sick from all of it."

Portions of Mr. Temple's story silently repeated themselves. *Charlie had talked and talked. He'd sung, and he was wounded!*

"Mr. Temple," Glory said, "you say the deputy left, but he wasn't at home when we left Winkler, and we didn't pass his truck on the road. Do you know where he went?"

"'Deed I don't. I thought maybe he was going to a hospital, because Jessie was passed out and we couldn't get her to come to. We thought at first she was dead, but he said she was still breathing. When we couldn't get her to wake up he put her in the truck. Took the kids with him too. The sheriff come a little while ago. He said likely the deputy took her to the jail in Marlinton."

"Oh, my," I said. "What will happen to the children?"

Mr. Temple nodded. "That's sad business. Jessie was trying to take care of them little kids, but I don't think she had near enough to feed them. We tried to help, but folks here don't hardly have enough to feed theirselves. Since her granddaughter passed, Jessie's been alone in the world, just her and her granddaughter's kids."

Glory wrote her name and telephone number on an envelope from her purse and gave it to Mr. Temple. "Please call us if you know of something we can do for Jessie's family."

He shook his head. "Ma'am, I'd say that family's done for."

Randolph reached into his pocket and pressed something into Mr. Temple's palm. "Please give this to Jessie's family, or anyone in need. Thanks for being a good neighbor."

Freddy stepped forward and gave him the bag of peanuts. "This isn't much, but maybe it will do somebody good. Merry Christmas."

I wished I had brought something to give.

CHAPTER 10

"So now we know," Randolph said, as we made our way down the steep road, prodding our umbrella tips and walking sticks in the wet mix of stones and clay to keep from slipping. "We know why Charlie couldn't call and why he didn't come home as expected."

I was glad for the sudden, cooler breeze, because the shock of Charlie's ordeal had left me hot and breathless.

"We still don't know if he went to Marlinton when he left here," Glory said. "But I suppose we can depend on him to come home. He might even call when he gets near a telephone."

"He's got a wound of some kind," Freddy said. "If he's smart, he'll see a doctor soon."

Charlie was plenty smart, though not always in the way everyone expected. I couldn't stop thinking about what Mr. Temple had said, that Charlie had talked and talked, possibly for hours. *Possibly for days.* And he'd sung "Jingle Bells." I'd never heard Charlie sing.

"I'm glad we came," Glory said. "We eased our minds, and we learned things he'd never tell us."

She was right. Our love and trust, that's all we needed to give Charlie, though I'd never seen evidence that he wanted either.

When we reached Winkler, Randolph took me home first. Freddy said he'd go back to the store. "Dad has vowed to close the doors at seven, no matter if everyone has been served or not. So we'll be home shortly after then."

"Do what you can to hurry him along," I said. "But I doubt he'll close as long as anyone is waiting to be served. A sign on the door might help. If you write 'Closing at six-thirty', then maybe you'll be able to close by seven." I knew it was hard to deny a customer, especially the night before Christmas.

"We'll try. If Tom comes home before I do, ask him to set the tree inside so it can dry," he said. "We'll decorate it tonight."

I climbed the steps to the porch with a subdued feeling of joy. I didn't know where Charlie was, but I had a shaky new confidence. He was like nobody else, and I should never doubt him.

Inside, I took off my muddy shoes and damp stockings and put on my ragged house shoes. Then I phoned Wanda and briefly described what we'd found. "Then maybe we'll see him soon," she said. "When Otis wakes up, tell him to go to Charlie's house and build a fire in his furnace."

"We're going to have a wonderful Christmas," I said.

"We will for sure. Is Aunt Piney behaving herself?"

"I haven't heard anything. She and Wanda Rose were going to bake our pies."

"That'll be a good one. Wanda Rose has never baked a pie in her life."

"Maybe Piney will come through," I said.

"It don't matter. You found out about Charlie, so I don't care if there's pie or not. Can you send one of the kids to fetch me home at six or should I set out walking?"

"I'll send someone." We'd often walked from one end of town to the other, but after a hard day's work, we needed a ride.

The house was quiet, likely Otis still asleep and Dessie

napping too. I heated up the morning coffee and fried a slice of our Christmas ham. Then with the ham sandwiched between two slices of yesterday's bread, I sat at the table and propped my feet on a chair. What a story I'd have to tell Barlow. And maybe when we saw Charlie he'd be willing to tell us the end of it.

~

I WOKE WHEN THE PHONE RANG, SURPRISED TO FIND MYSELF asleep on the hard kitchen chair, my rear numb, and my legs propped up and stiff. I'd eaten most of the sandwich but drunk only a sip of coffee. What remained in the cup was stone cold.

The caller was Wanda Rose. "Me and Aunt Piney's in a mess with your pies," she said. "The dough falls apart every time we try to lift it into the pan. Can we bring it all back to you?"

The clock struck three. "Do that," I said. "Is Piney better?"

"She's had a good afternoon. You may have to let her roll out the dough."

"Gladly."

We'd planned three pies, two apple and one mincemeat, but after hearing that Charlie had mentioned pumpkin as his favorite, I decided to make two of those as well. I measured flour for five pies into a metal washpan and went to the basement for canned pumpkin.

Dessie wandered into the kitchen, surprised to see me. She was eager for a report of our trip to Jennie Town, so while she mixed a molded gelatin, I described our adventure.

"I feel bad for the old woman," she said. "And them poor kids. Do you know how old they is?"

"I only know they're the woman's great-grandkids. The neighbor thinks they have no other folks."

"What they gonna do if their granny's put in jail?"

I shook my head. Maybe someone would take them in.

"It's sad to think about, especially at Christmas," Dessie said.

The troubles and despairs of others seemed sadder at times when we believed everyone should be rejoicing, but in their present circumstances, I doubted the season mattered much to those children.

Dessie asked, "So why have you got that bunch of flour in the washpan?"

"I decided to make five pies. Wanda Rose and Piney are coming back. Their attempts with my piecrust failed, so we'll start over. Wanda Rose suggested I let Piney roll out the crusts, but I'll need you to do the lattice, please." I could never do lattice as well as Dessie and Tom.

"You're making pumpkin too?"

"For Charlie," I said. "I'm hoping he'll be here after all."

She smiled in support of my foolish hope.

The rest of the afternoon passed quickly, with Piney contentedly following our orders to sprinkle cinnamon or roll the dough I set before her. I stood back, watching the contented look on her face as she rolled the pin. "Doing fine," I said. And she was.

As soon as the pies were out of the oven, I set in two pans of cornbread to go with our evening meal of vegetable soup. Everyone would be hungry, so we didn't need anything fancy, just a lot of something that tasted good.

"The kids is gonna want to cut into one o'them pies," Dessie said.

"The pies are too warm to cut, and I do hope to save them for tomorrow. Maybe I can hold them off with candy."

"You made candy?"

"I asked Hettie to bring a couple of boxes of chocolates from the store." This year my Christmas traditions had fallen apart. I'd been so busy with school lessons and the school program that I hadn't made cookies or candy. "Maybe after Christmas we can get the children to make peanut brittle. Oh, I forgot. Hettie wants spiced cider tonight when they decorate the tree. We should have cookies. Is there time to make some?"

"No need," Dessie said. "I forgot something too. Jonah Jr. dropped off a platter of Christmas cookies from his mom. They're on the dining room table."

"I'd relish a cookie now," Piney said. "Everything goes better with a cookie."

"We should make cookies to take to those poor old folks in Beauty," Dessie said.

It was a fine idea. Maybe I'd send the cookies with Charlie.

CHAPTER 11

My wrapped Christmas gifts were stacked in a corner of the bedroom. In the kitchen, five pies cooled on the worktable, and the ham was ready to bake tomorrow. I thought I had everything under control. I thought I had *myself* under control, but my stomach began to churn with anxiety, late in the afternoon, when snow started to fall in fat wet flakes. Everyone professed to love a white Christmas, but someone I loved was somewhere on the road, and snow like this made roads treacherous.

There'd been ample time for Charlie to take the poor old woman and her grandkids to Marlinton and return home. I rang his number again but of course there was no answer.

The heavy snow soon dampened all sounds outside. Inside, our house was also quiet, Dessie having a lie-down in her room and Piney dozing at the kitchen table. Wanda Rose sat across from her, pensive, occasionally writing a word or two in a notebook.

"Your friends will be sledding on the schoolhouse hill," I said. "You should go."

She nodded. "Maybe later."

"There's nothing to do until supper. We appreciate your help, but we want you to enjoy yourself, too."

"I'm waiting for Otis to wake up," she said. "Maybe he'll go sledding with me."

I'd just taken the cornbread out of the oven when Otis came bounding down the back stairs into the kitchen.

"About time," Wanda Rose said.

He gave her shoulder a playful punch, then picked a crumb from the edge of an apple pie and popped it in his mouth. "What's to eat?"

"Not that," I said. "Warm cornbread and vegetable soup. Since you slept through lunch, you may have your dinner now."

Quietly he slid a chair from the table. Piney slept on as he buttered his cornbread, which crumbled because it was too fresh to cut. He scooped up the crumbs and put them in his soup. He ate quickly, like he had somewhere to be.

Wanda Rose asked, "You're going back to the hospital?" She didn't mention sledding.

"Yeah. I'll bring Mom home and I'll work tonight if they need me." He nodded toward the worktable. "There's a lot of pie. Couldn't I have mine now? I'll take any kind. Warm pie, stale pie, old moldy pie." He gave us a beseeching smile.

Wanda Rose saved me from having to refuse. "There's never stale or moldy pie in this house, and these pies will not be cut until dinner tomorrow. Sorry, if you're not here you might not get any."

"I'll hide a slice for you," I said. "Remember, we're trimming the tree tonight. There'll be cookies and spiced cider."

"I'll try to make it."

"Oh, come on, Otis," Wanda Rose said. "I never get to see you. I should be more important than a bunch of strangers at the hospital."

"They're not all strangers," he said. "One is Aunt Blanche. And I don't have many chances to work with Dr. Madison. He talks a lot about Dad. You should get a job at the hospital, Sissy, if you still fancy being a doctor."

"Well fancy this," she said. "Mom lets you work at the hospital, but she won't let me."

"Your time will come." Rising from the table, he punched his sister's shoulder. "I missed you, kid."

"Then don't miss me tonight! Come home!"

"Do my best." He shrugged on a jacket, set an oiled rain hat over his curly hair and stepped outside. Then he stepped back in. "Hey, it's coming down hard out there. *Snow*, not rain."

"We know, stupid," Wanda Rose said.

With a wink, he shut the door behind him.

Wanda Rose pouted. "Otis is no fun anymore. College did that to him, got him into books and medicine and away from how he was."

"Otis is an older version of himself, that's all," I said. "Most likely you'll be different, too, in a few years."

She closed her notebook. "I don't want to be different. I don't want any of us to change."

I carried the soup bowl and utensils to the sink and wiped crumbs from the table, wondering if I should let her declaration pass without comment. Most young people were eager for change. It was mothers like Wanda and me who wanted to stop the passage of time.

Wanda Rose was a wise child, but perhaps too attached to the family, though that attachment was good for us. She was a delightful young woman, full of piss and vinegar, as her Aunt Piney had once observed. But in the past year she seemed to have lost interest in people her own age. One thing I knew: I shouldn't lecture, and whatever I said shouldn't sound like criticism.

"Change is like fire," I said. "Sometimes it's good, and sometimes devastating. A lot of the time we don't see it coming, so all we can do is try to manage it. You might say that's what Otis is about these days. He's trying to stop bad changes from happening by learning about changes that will be good."

"Like medicine."

I nodded. "We all need to know more. You and Otis are like your father—he was always learning, and always looking for a way to make things better. He left a great heritage, not just who he was as a doctor or how he rebuilt this town, but his paintings: a history of the valley, this town, and his family."

"I miss him," she said.

"Of course; we all do." This girl had not visibly grieved her father's death. He'd been gone for years, but his was the first time I'd heard her acknowledge her loss.

"It'd be nice if Uncle Charlie came around more often."

"I agree. He said he'd be here for Christmas dinner. He might be home now, out seeing to his horses."

"I could saddle up Hustler and ride over to see," she said.

I sighed in relief. "If you would, please." I was afraid she'd caught a gloomy spirit from me. She needed to get out, away from the care of an addled old woman and worries like mine and her mother's. "Does Hustler mind the snow?"

"He loves it. So do I," she said.

"Then don't tarry. If you find Charlie, just tell him we're expecting him for dinner tomorrow. Tell him he's welcome to come tonight, too, for dinner and tree decorating."

"You'll have to keep an eye on Aunt Piney," she said.

"I'll do that. Be careful, don't hurry the horse. And wrap up good. And if you want to stop and see friends, just give us a call so we'll know."

"Yes, Granny." I was pleased to hear her laugh.

In the next hour, Dessie and Piney woke and sat at the table with cups of hot sugared tea. Dessie told stories of people they'd known, encouraging Piney to remember. When they were girls, there'd been no Winkler, but they remembered a trading post here. Their families had attended the same one-room school, a few miles up in the hills.

I kept thinking Charlie might call. The party line rang a lot that afternoon, and finally I heard our three short rings. The caller was Glory. Without wasting time for greetings or pleasantries, she said, "Is there news?"

"Here's the news: I'm going to call the sheriff."

"Good. Call me back. I'm at the shop. Randolph and Johnny are taking care of Christmas decorating and Christmas dinner."

"Randolph is cooking?"

"Everything will be fine. He says if he gets in trouble, he'll consult a book. Or call you."

I shouldn't have been surprised; Randolph could figure out anything. He'd developed and managed coal mines, our telephone system and our power station. Glory's shop now had electric machines, and he maintained those, too. On the surface, their marriage seemed happy, and I hoped that was true. She'd always been strongly independent, and had resisted Randolph's proposals for many years before giving in.

"You're a lucky girl," I said, "but don't be reckless. Go home before the snow piles up."

"It's snowing?"

"Go home," I said. "I'll call you there."

It was past time to call the sheriff.

CHAPTER 12

"Never passed Charlie on the road," the sheriff said, "and I can't find no sign he ever brought that woman and her kids to Marlinton. I looked all over: the jail, the hospital, and I spoke to some who know him. Might be the kids told him about family somewhere and he took them there. I wouldn't worry. Likely he's on his way home right now."

"It's snowing," I said. "And it's foggy." I couldn't see anything past our front porch. I regretted that I'd let Wanda Rose ride the two miles to Charlie's house, but it hadn't been foggy then. Still, the town was small, and we knew it so well we could find our way in the dark.

"Snowing here too," the sheriff said. "Don't worry, Missus. Charlie always turns up and he always does the right thing. Likely he's off doing that right now, finding them kids' family."

"That would be good," I said. "If you see him, will you ask him to please call home?"

"Sure will. You and your family have a nice Christmas, now."

I wished the sheriff a Merry Christmas, but my heart wasn't in it. Pieces of my heart were attached to my loved ones, wherever they were. It was an unreasonable sensation, brought on by the one who was missing.

By six, the fog was a silvery mist in the dark. Wanda Rose returned, wet and breathless. "It's slippery as snot out there," she said, coming in from the back porch. "Town's busy, though. Cars and wagons parked along the street. Aunt Glory's car is pulled over at the bottom of the road up to her house. Guess that means she had to walk up the hill."

"Will our car make it home?" Trudging through the snow would be hard for Barlow, especially after a long day like this one.

"Folks are getting around. Aunt Glory's not a very good driver, don't you know." Wanda Rose stepped to the stove and stirred the soup. "When are we gonna eat?"

"Soon as the others are home."

At the table, Piney held up a cutout of a silver star. "Look, how pretty."

"Very pretty," Wanda Rose said.

For the past hour, Dessie and Piney had been working at the table with a stack of last year's Christmas cards, making paper ornaments to hang on our tree. Encouraged by Dessie, Piney cut slowly around images of Santa Claus, angels, and stars. For each cutout, Dessie punched a hole in the paper and looped a string through it.

"Very pretty," Wanda Rose said. "Will we dress up for dinner?"

I'd brought two jugs of cider from the cellar so I could honor Hettie's request, but beyond that, my only idea about this evening was a wish for good news about Charlie and for Piney to remain calm.

We'd started wearing our winter best on Christmas Eve for the service at the church, though what we wore hardly mattered because usually the church was cold, and we kept our coats on. Then we'd come home and have spiced cider and decorate the tree. In recent years there'd been no Christmas Eve service at the church. Some complained that by emphasizing Santa Claus and making Christmas an event for family celebrations we'd thrown out the meaning of Christmas. But Wanda approved the change, saying everyone needed that night to prepare for Christmas day, and Barlow was also glad he didn't have to go out again after a long day of serving Christmas shoppers. We still decorated the tree on Christmas Eve, and we'd kept the tradition of dressing up.

I glanced down at my faded skirt and broken-down house shoes. "I won't cheer anyone looking like this. So yes, I'll wear the green dress Glory gave me last year. But everyone can do what they like." I no longer had the privilege or the responsibility of telling my children what to wear.

"Then I'll tell everyone to dress up," Wanda Rose said.

The older ones among us might have benefitted from an early bedtime, I realized, when Otis brought Wanda from her day's work at the hospital. Slowly she unwrapped her scarf and held it toward a wall hook, missing the mark. The scarf fell to the floor. Otis swept it up, helped her off with her coat and playfully plucked her hat from her head. "Thank you," she mumbled. "Ten hours on my feet, half the time in a rush. Can't wait to get out of these shoes."

"Is it raining now?" Their hats, scarves, and the shoulders of their coats were wet.

"It's a mix," Otis said. "The snow's turned to mush. Let's hope it doesn't freeze tonight."

"Yes, let's hope." I said that word too much, as though I lived on it instead of trust and faith. "Wanda, why not lie down for an hour? Piney's content where she is, and there's nothing to do for supper but wait."

"Good. Call me." She trudged up the stairs.

An hour later, Barlow, Freddy and Hettie arrived from work. I'd washed my face and changed into the green dress. I was rewarded by approval in my husband's eyes.

"All you have to do now is rest and enjoy," I whispered, as he took off his overcoat. "Are you ready for dinner or would you like to change?"

He smiled, but his eyes drooped and his movements were slow. "I'll change," he said, "because you look so nice."

"Come, then." I put my arm through his and walked with him to the apartment.

"I don't suppose there's time for a bath?"

"The sooner we start on this evening the sooner it will be over," I said.

"So no bath."

"If you want a bath, we can wait dinner."

"Don't do that."

I found his best shirt, the one with French cuffs.

"You might lie down for a few minutes," I said. "Wanda had a nap."

"Dinner will perk me up. And you." He wrapped his arms around me and pressed his cheek against mine. His face was cold and damp. "Ah, see? I'm restored now."

I pretended to agree. "Do you want a jacket or sweater?"

"Do I have a nice sweater?"

I opened a drawer and took out the one I'd given him last Christmas, a gray cardigan with specks of red. In the same drawer was a black bow tie.

"I don't think I've ever worn that tie," he said.

"Then it will be special."

He sat patiently on the edge of the bed as I fussed with the ends of the tie. "I guess you haven't heard from Charlie," he said.

"Nothing. The sheriff is now certain he didn't take that woman to Marlinton. Barlow, your shoes look like they're soaked through. You should change."

He bent and unlaced his shoes. "Stockings, too," I said. Slowly he peeled them off.

His feet were red and looked cold. I took his hand. It was

cold, too. "I can always bring your supper on a tray. You can join us in the parlor later."

"May Rose, I'm fine. And Charlie's fine, too, wherever he is. Please don't fuss. Worrying won't help."

I brought dry stockings and his Sunday shoes. "I've stopped worrying. I don't think Charlie's ever been with us for Christmas Eve, so why should this night be different?"

He took my hands in his. "Let's appreciate the ones who are here. I'm tired, but this was a great day. Hettie and Freddy must have waited on four customers to my one. Maybe I was slow because I couldn't stop watching them—it's rare to see them interacting with others. May Rose, our children are grown up."

"I know." His confirmation of my feeling was both sad and happy, a true example of the word *bittersweet*. "Are you sure you don't want to lie back for 15 minutes?"

"I'll rest tomorrow." He pulled on the dry stockings and shoes, and I helped him into the sleeves of his sweater.

"After the holidays, let's talk about the store," I said. "You might let someone else manage it. Or find a buyer?" We'd imagined such a time, years ago, but now that the need for this change in our lives was greater, it was hard to talk about.

"It's something to consider. I don't like you being so tired, either. If I give up the store, maybe you should stop teaching."

"Maybe I will." In a few days—in the new year—we'd consider new directions. For tonight, Hettie wanted spiced cider and Wanda Rose wanted Otis with us, and she wanted everyone to dress up. I wanted all of us to be together. We all wanted Blanche to get well and Piney to have a pleasant time. We also wanted Piney to return to her old dependable self, but we knew that was a vain hope. Nothing stayed the same.

Our dinner wasn't fancy, but there was a lot of it, and we all had healthy appetites, even Otis, who'd eaten just two hours earlier. I admired how festive everyone looked, especially Hettie in a red wool dress with long sleeves and a flared skirt, and Wanda

Rose in a pink angora sweater and slim dark skirt. Dessie had found a red ribbon for Piney's hair, and Freddy had found a red bow tie. Dessie wore her garnet necklace, and Barlow's gold cufflinks sparkled at his wrists.

Barlow had brought home a jug of fruit liquor, a gift from a customer, and he now poured small glasses for everyone, including the youngest, Wanda Rose.

Lifting his glass, Tom said, "What a sight for old eyes, all you good-looking young folks at the table."

Barlow cleared his throat. "Don't forget us handsome, mature fellows." He raised his glass and looked at me. "And our beautiful ladies."

"Amen," Otis said.

As most of us were taking our first sip, Piney covered her face and began to utter deep breathy sobs.

"Oh, sweetheart," Wanda said. "What can I do? Do you want to go home?" Piney cried harder, and Wanda stood, preparing to take her from the room.

"Wanda," I said, "Let's have some Christmas songs."

"Now?"

I glanced toward Piney. "A song may help."

When Wanda shook her head *no*, I said, "Wanda Rose, what's your favorite Christmas song?"

She gave me a look of surprise. "The one about the Christmas tree?"

"That's nice. Will you sing it for us?" Wanda Rose's voice was almost as strong as her mother's.

She glanced toward Piney, then at her mother and back to me. "I guess. Do you want me to sing right here?" Our children had never been allowed to sing or read at the table.

"Stand or sit, whatever you like."

"I'll probably need help with the words."

"Maybe not here," Barlow said, starting to rise. "Shall we all go to the parlor?"

"Here, please," I said. "Some of us are still eating."

Obediently he sat. "Whatever you say."

"Hum along, everyone, or sing if you like. Then we'll finish eating and us old folks will find the best seats in the parlor and watch the tree trimming."

At the first words of "O Christmas Tree", Wanda Rose's young voice was drowned out by Piney's sobs. Then Wanda began to hum and Wanda Rose sang louder. Finally Tom, Hettie and Otis joined in. Piney stopped crying, and a gradual smile of peace spread over her face.

When the song ended, Piney clapped. "Now let's have Jingle Bells!"

CHAPTER 13

The bare tree and its lovely scent of pine waited for us in the parlor. Before dinner, Otis and Freddy had found the wooden frame we used each year to support the tree and the square washtub we set it in.

Wanda took Piney to a chair with a good view and sat beside her, holding her hand, and I went to fetch a sheet to conceal the washtub. When I returned, someone had strewn the floor with our boxes of old ornaments.

If not for the need to distract Piney, we might have cleared the dining table and washed dishes before gathering in the parlor, but being both full and tired, I didn't care if those tasks waited until morning. Dessie and Tom sat on the loveseat, and I sat in a wing chair beside Barlow, who looked like he might immediately fall asleep, despite bursts of hilarity among our young people. I smiled and told myself I didn't need to know their jokes or their secrets.

What a long day it had been, with the excursion to Jennie Town, the pie baking, and so many calls about Charlie. Wanda and I had not yet had a moment alone, so I hadn't told her about my conversation with the sheriff. My good shoes felt tight on my feet, and I wished I could exchange them for my scuffed, broken-down house shoes. Or soothe my feet in a pan of hot water. Endure, I told myself. Soon there would be rest. Everything would work out.

Meanwhile, our young people strung lights on the tree and hung Piney's cutouts and our old ornaments. Tom went to the kitchen and brought back cups of the spiced cider that had been warming on the stove, and Wanda carried in Bertha Watson's platter of cookies.

We murmured our delight when Freddy plugged in the lights.

"Freddy," I said. "Do you remember when you recited 'The Night Before Christmas' for the school program?"

"Can't forget it," he said. "It's a recurring nightmare, comes whenever I'm worried about something I have to do."

"Oh, I'm sorry. I didn't think you hated it."

"It's all right Ma. I didn't hate it."

"Darn right you didn't," Hettie said. "You were puffed up proud."

"I was going to ask if you'd recite it for us now."

He shook his head. "I remember the first line, *'Twas the Night Before Christmas.* There you are."

"I hope you never felt forced to perform," I said. "You memorized the poem when you were six. I always thought it was too much for a child your age."

"Oh, Hettie's right, I was proud at the time. But I was always anxious about it too. I'm not a performer. I don't like to make speeches or anything like that," he said.

Hettie persisted. "I don't see how you could forget the words, seeing as how you recited it every year. I mean, nobody else had a chance until you went to high school. It got to be a tradition."

"And now an embarrassing memory," he laughed.

"Baloney. Stand here," she said, arranging Wanda Rose, Otis and Freddy beside her in front of the tree. "We'll say it together. The rest of you can jump in with the words if we get stuck."

Raggedly, they struggled through the poem, Freddy contributing most of the words. There was a lot of laughter among them, and I laughed and sniffed back my own memories.

We clapped at the end, and our young people bowed. Then Hettie said to Freddy, "Don't let anybody move." She and Wanda Rose left the room.

Barlow's eyes closed and his face relaxed, and Dessie and Tom also seemed comfortable. I thought about the remnants of vegetable soup drying on dishes left on the table.

The girls returned with stacks of wrapped gifts, which they put under the tree.

"Mom," Hettie said. "May I give you my present now?"

She'd always begged to open her own gifts on Christmas Eve. I was about to say she could not, but I suspected something different in her request. "I wouldn't mind, but would others? Don't we want to save the gifts until tomorrow?"

"Just mine," Hettie said to everyone. "I want to give Mom and Dad my gifts now."

"Fine with me," Dessie said. "Let's have a look."

Hettie placed her gifts on our laps, and everyone watched as we unwrapped them. "Oh," I said, opening the lid of a shoebox and pulling out a house shoe in soft green leather. It had a flat sole and a flannel lining. I slid my hand into it, feeling the comfort. Barlow's box contained house shoes too, brown leather, also with a warm flannel lining.

"I thought you might like to wear them tomorrow morning," she said. "Or now."

"Now," Barlow grunted, untying his Sunday shoes. When the new slippers were on his feet, he placed his shoes in the gift box, sighing loudly so everyone would see how pleased he was. I sighed, too, as my pinched toes spread out in the welcome comfort of our daughter's thoughtful gift.

Unexpectedly, Piney began to sing "O Christmas Tree." Her

voice was weak but true. Like the others, I watched and listened in awe, because I'd never heard her sing alone.

"How beautiful," I said, when her voice faded on the last words.

Piney tugged on Wanda's hand. "Sing the next verse, I forget how it goes."

Obediently Wanda sang,

> *O Christmas Tree, O Christmas tree,*
> *Of all the trees most lovely;*
> *O Christmas Tree, O Christmas tree,*
> *Of all the trees most lovely.*
> *Each year you bring to us delight...*

Her voice broke, and she turned her head and swiped at her cheeks. Normally, Wanda's sadness came out in spurts of anger and irritation. We were used to that. Her tears were harder to witness.

"Please don't cry," Piney said. "It was real pretty."

Wanda cleared her throat. "Time for bed, Aunt Piney. Shall we go up together?"

"I'm sleeping here?"

"Just for tonight," Wanda said. "So we'll all be together Christmas morning."

"Blanche and Charlie too," Piney said.

Wanda nodded. The room was quiet, everyone attentive to Piney. Then we shifted our attention to Otis, who'd put his coat over his arm. "This was nice. Thanks for the great dinner and a good time. I'll see you all tomorrow morning."

Piney said, "Where's he going?"

Wanda helped her up from her chair. "He's going to the hospital. He'll check on Blanche for us."

Suddenly frantic, Piney looked around the room. "Where did she go?"

"She's at the hospital now," Wanda said. "She was sick, remember? She's getting better there. She'll come home soon."

Piney's face relaxed. "Oh, yes. You shouldn't worry, Blanche is tough. She'll be home soon. And Charlie. Him and her is good children, so good to me and her pa."

"Indeed they are," I said.

Piney waved. "Excuse me, I need my bed. I'm...I'm... *Dusty!*"

Nobody laughed, but our smiles were sweet.

CHAPTER 14

Our young people had magically erased my fatigue and apprehensions with songs and memories of Christmases past, but no magic had cleaned the dishes. They attacked this problem with a lot of hilarity, insisting I sit at the table and observe their expertise as they managed the final task of the day. I was glad to agree, happy to sit back and study them, something that at any other time felt invasive and nosey. Silently I approved their quick hands, laughing eyes and lovely smooth skin. I did not always understand their references, but I loved how they teased and nudged. I counted my blessings.

Wanda returned as they were setting the clean dishes in the cupboard and wiping down the sink and worktable. "Piney fell asleep soon as she hit the bed," she said.

"I love her," Hettie said. The others agreed, there was no one better than Piney. We did not speak of her challenges.

I had not told most of the family about my most recent news—or lack of it—about Charlie, and Wanda asked for it now. "So Ma, did you call the sheriff about Charlie?"

Wanda Rose, Freddie and Hettie paused their chatter and listened. I could only tell them where Charlie was not: not at home, no longer at the old camp above Jennie Town, and not in Marlinton. Not stuck somewhere on the road, I hoped.

"If he doesn't show up tomorrow, I can drive north and ask about him along the way," Freddy said.

"He'd hate that," Wanda Rose said.

"Too bad," Freddy said. "The family needs some information."

Wanda Rose was right: Charlie would not want us to ask people about him. He'd never said as much, but I sensed he did not like people talking or even thinking about him. I might have to tell him about all the talk and concern he'd caused by neglecting to make a simple telephone call.

On my way to bed I answered another call from Glory. "Just checking," she said.

"We shouldn't worry."

"I know," she said. "Did you have a good evening? How's Blanche?"

"Wanda says she's improving, and yes, we had a lovely evening. Otis is working at the hospital tonight."

"I'm eager to see everyone. If it's all right with you, we'll come for a visit tomorrow afternoon."

Glory had grown up without knowing her brothers, and ever since they'd relocated to Winkler, I'd watched her attempts to reunite the family. I knew she wanted to understand Charlie and be understood by him, and she wanted to know more about their parents. Charlie had been too young to remember his mother, but I was sure he had strong memories of their father, as did I. Neither Charlie nor Will had professed to remember anything about their father except his skills as an artist, and Barlow and I also pretended we hadn't known much about him.

There were subjects and people I did not like to think about because the memories were too disturbing, but perhaps my avoidance was wrong. Maybe there was a broader truth about Morris Herff. At one time he'd been an innocent child; we knew nothing about that. We'd condemned him because he'd abused his children with neglect, and based on that information, we'd erased his history from the family. Perhaps that wasn't fair.

I'd tried to tell Glory there were always people we wished we knew better, people who for some reason or other never returned our feelings. I'd said that closeness didn't seem to be possible for Charlie, that the only differences between his feelings for family and strangers might be his regular gifts of grain or a horse and the help he furnished when it was needed most. He never confided. He never gave us a chance to reciprocate by helping him, because he didn't seem to need or care about what we could do. Still, he was devoted to us, I was sure.

"We won't come until after your nap," Glory laughed. "Say about three o'clock?"

Visitors at three? Three was too close to dinner. "Tomorrow we're eating at four. Would you like to join us?"

"Thank you, but Randolph and Johnny have planned..." Her voice cut off.

"Woops," someone said. It was Wanda, still in the kitchen.

In darkness, I held onto the telephone earpiece. Our electricity had gone out, and the phone line was dead. I stood still, waiting for my eyes to adjust to the dark, orienting myself by the lighter rectangle that was the window of our front door.

"I got the lantern. Who's got a match?" *That was Freddy.* He must have found the lantern we kept on a hook inside the cellar door.

"There's matches on the shelf over the woodstove." *Hettie's voice.*

"Found them." That was Wanda Rose.

I replaced the earpiece on the hook and waited for my eyes to adjust to the dark. A shadow moved across the lighter rectangle of the front door window. Tom said, "Anyone out here?"

Then someone brought light into the hallway. Freddy and I saw each other in the light of his raised lantern.

In the next minutes, we found and lit all our lamps and

lanterns, which we set in the kitchen, parlor, my sitting room, the upstairs hallway, and Piney's room, in case she woke and was frightened in the dark.

"Likely ice brought the electric and phone lines down somewhere," Tom said. "Randolph will be going out to see. Fred, you want to help?"

"Might as well," Freddy said.

They left, dressed in coats, boots, caps and gloves, each with a lantern, promising they would not touch a wire until they were certain that Randolph had turned off the generator in the power plant.

Wanda and I followed them as far as the porch and watched as they got into Tom's truck and drove down the lane. It was a beautiful night, quiet and sparkling, but likely not appreciated by anyone without a warm shelter.

"That place we went today, looking for Charlie, it's just a pile of shacks," I said.

"Yeah. I lived in a place like that with my ma before we came to Winkle," Wanda said.

"The woman's neighbor said the children didn't have enough to eat. I hate hearing about such things."

I'd lived rough, too, with Jamie Long, the husband I was happy to forget. In our two years together we'd had no Christmas celebration. One of those winters, Jamie had not even come home. To keep my sanity, I'd sung and talked to myself.

"Someone is always suffering," Wanda said. "Even the rich get sick, and they grieve too, just like the poor."

"Those children have no mother. If the old woman goes to jail, they'll have no one."

"Poor little things."

"It's hard to believe what Mr. Temple said about Charlie talking so much to that old woman," I said. "And singing! Then how he took her away with him. And the children. Can you imagine?"

"It's what you'd have done," Wanda said.

"And you." I hadn't shared with anyone my recurring twinge of fear that Jessie might have wakened in the truck and caused more trouble. Maybe we were all worrying about the same possibility.

I tested the wooden surface of the top porch step and found its invisible coat of ice. There was nothing to do but have faith that Randolph, Tom and Freddy would find the broken wires without stepping on them. And that Charlie was warm and safe. Someday we'd know more about it, though I was certain we'd never know everything, only the portion he chose to tell.

That night as I tried to sleep, I wished I'd been able to go to bed immediately after the singing and the kitchen fun, soothed by memories and sweet sounds, not these new anxieties. I was wakeful for hours, wondering if Charlie was somewhere in trouble.

CHAPTER 15

When I woke on Christmas morning our house was warm, meaning someone had recently added coal to the furnace. I was sure it wasn't Barlow, who looked as though he had not moved. He was so still, I bent close to reassure myself that he was breathing. We really did need to talk about the store. Barlow would never close it without someone to take it over. As the only general store in Winkler, it was necessary.

Turning a lamp switch produced no light, but the oil lamp in my sitting room gave off a yellow glow and threw shadows to the corners. The lamp in the parlor and the kitchen lantern still burned too, though the flames were low.

Someone had also built up the fire in the woodstove, so I put water in the percolator, measured coffee into the basket, and set the pot at the back of the stove to brew slowly. Then I carried the lantern to the basement and found a tin of lamp oil, half full, and a few new wicks. If the electric lines were not repaired soon, people would need Tom to open the filling station so they could buy oil for their lamps and lanterns.

As though responding to my thoughts, Tom came into the

kitchen as I was cleaning the lamp. "Smelled coffee," he said quietly.

"Sorry, I hope I didn't wake you too soon."

"I been up a while." He took mugs from the cupboard and stood by the stove, judging the color and aroma of the coffee as it perked through the glass knob on the lid.

"Did you and Freddy work all night?"

"Not long. We found some broken lines, but Randolph didn't want to try fixing them in the dark. We're going out soon as it gets light."

"I'm glad you can help, but I'm sorry you'll miss your day of rest."

Laughing, Tom poured his coffee and opened the refrigerator for milk. "Plenty of time for that when I'm dead."

I had no smile for his joke. I didn't know Tom's age, but I knew he and Dessie had been married almost 40 years, because their marriage dated back to the year I'd met Barlow. My years with Barlow were only a little more than half of their years together but they were my best ones, and I wanted more of them. I hoped Barlow would agree we should be together all day, every day. It was time for him to take life easy, if there could be such a thing.

"Tom," I said. "Is Charlie a good driver?"

His eyes widened in surprise. "Don't know, I never rode with him. I guess he's good as most, but I don't think he drives much." He laughed. "He forgets about the gas. He's run out a time or two."

Running out of gas was something I hadn't considered. In these hills, gasoline filling stations were even farther apart than our little towns. I wished I hadn't asked.

Without electricity, I felt slightly off-kilter, but we'd lived without it before, and were lucky we still had the old wood cooker. I took our bottle of milk from the warm refrigerator and set it on the back porch to chill.

"Would you like bacon? If you're going to work in this cold, you should eat something hearty now."

We'd planned a late, casual breakfast at ten, a buffet that wouldn't require much time in the kitchen: coffee, eggs (boiled yesterday) oranges, milk and puffed wheat.

"Bacon would be good," Tom said. "I'll cut a few slices, some for Freddy too."

"There's yesterday's bread." I hadn't planned to bake today, but now I decided to make dinner rolls. I set the canister of flour on the worktable. The dough would rise quickly in the warm kitchen and the rolls would soon be ready for the oven.

I started mixing the dough while Tom fried bacon. Freddy came down the back stairs, drawn, he said, by the aroma of sizzling bacon. They made bacon sandwiches and sat and ate together.

"I hope we'll finish in time for dinner," Tom said.

"Dinner's at four," I reminded him. "You mean the repairs could take all day?"

"Don't really know. I guess it's possible."

So they might not return in time for our morning exchange of gifts. I was ashamed of my disappointment. "Randolph and Glory have no woodstove, so he'll have no way to cook their dinner unless he mends the lines soon."

"Nothing will be fixed right away. Repairs will take hours," Freddy said.

"Then tell Randolph to bring his family and eat with us at four, even if the lines aren't repaired by then."

"If Randolph approves, I'll round up some fellows to help," Freddy said. "We should finish by dinnertime."

"Gifts tonight, then, instead of this morning," I said. "And Freddy?"

"Yes?"

"Before you do anything, would you go to Piney's and Charlie's houses and fire their furnaces? And put some hay down for Piney's heifer."

"Will do," Freddy said. "We'll see Charlie today, Mom, I'm sure of it."

"Keep saying that." I needed his confidence.

After they left, Wanda came to the kitchen, and I described our altered plans for the day. Then Otis returned from the hospital, reporting that his night's work had been quiet, with only five patients. He and a nurse had managed adequately with lanterns. "Doc Madison says Blanche should come home in a couple of days. She's anxious about Charlie."

"She knows he's missing?" Blanche had given up on Charlie long ago, and as far as I could tell she'd been content to live quietly with Piney.

"Word gets around, you know," he said.

"Poor Blanche. We should take Christmas dinner to her."

"Maybe just dessert," Wanda said. "And we'll take Aunt Piney too."

The morning went on, everyone waking at a different time and coming to the kitchen for coffee, learning of our change of plans, and bless their hearts, asking if they could help. I set the dinner rolls to rise, and Wanda and I took turns checking on Piney, who'd decided to sit and admire the Christmas tree and the colorful packages arranged beneath it. Later I found Barlow sitting in the parlor too, listening to Hettie read *A Christmas Carol*.

I had so many reasons to be grateful.

CHAPTER 16

Before noon, our gray sky was brightened by sunshine. I went to the front porch and looked down the lane for signs of traffic. Icicles on the eaves dripped water and broke off. Holding onto the railing, I tested the top step and discovered the shine was only water.

As I watched, a horse and rider turned into our lane. I could see the rider wasn't Charlie, but maybe he was someone with news. He arrived with a request. "There's several folks at the filling station, needing kerosene. Any chance it's gonna open?"

Since Tom was working on the power lines, Barlow said he'd open the station and stay there until power was restored. I was glad he had this distraction. Maybe if he gave up the store, he could help Tom occasionally in the filling station.

Inside, sunshine streamed through the windows. I paused to admire the Christmas cards Wanda Rose and Hettie were taping to the woodwork around the parlor and dining room doors. Piney was helping by handing them the cards, but she set the cards down and followed me to the kitchen. "I don't know where Simpson has got to," she said.

She seemed satisfied when I said he might be out feeding the cattle. I felt guilty about our constant deceit, but when she was missing her husband, she couldn't manage the current reality. Most days our goal was to keep her calm. Blanche had been doing that before her sickness, I realized, without much help from us.

We'd saved the potatoes for Piney to peel, and she occupied herself with these. I put the ham in the oven to bake. There seemed little to do but wait for the electricity to be restored and the family to come home, but having little to do gave me too much time to think.

Years ago when Charlie left to follow his young dream of being a cowboy, I'd worried and waited for him to return. After a few years without a shred of news, I accepted what Wanda and others believed to be true. Charlie was dead. But Wanda's Uncle Russell never gave up, and finally he found him in a jail, beaten and broken, and brought him home to Winkler. Charlie had slowly recovered his memories, but in many ways he remained a stranger.

Did he know how important he was, and how we would feel if once again he disappeared without a word? I scolded myself for allowing such a thought. Our feelings didn't matter. He didn't want us to know him; he only wanted acceptance for the parts of himself he gave us. The only person who could reasonably be disturbed by Charlie's behavior was the one he'd married, and Blanche seemed to have given up on him years ago.

Our lights came on early in the afternoon, and almost immediately the telephone rang, a call from Glory, accepting our dinner invitation. When the phone rang again, Hettie ran to answer it. We could hear her from the kitchen as she stood in the hall, listening, talking, and laughing. This was the call she'd been waiting for. I had to agree with Wanda and Dessie: a new life for my daughter was underway.

We put away the oil lamps, extended the dining room table, and began to lay out plates.

Tom, Freddy, and Barlow returned, and since we had time on

our hands, Wanda suggested we take pie to Blanche. Since Otis had said there were five patients in the hospital, we cut seven pieces so we could share with the nurse and orderly. Piney was excited to go out in the sunshine, but protested wearing a coat, saying she was too warm already. Instead of arguing, we carried her coat outside, where the cold air made her agree to wear it. Wanda had wrapped a gift for Piney to give Blanche.

Piney happily carried the gift into the hospital, but she cried when she saw Blanche lying pale and still against the white sheets and white walls of the hospital ward. Her tears ended when she watched Blanche take the paper from her Christmas gift and press the soft red sweater to her cheek. After that, Piney helped us pass pie to the other patients, and insisted Blanche eat hers while we watched.

"I guess you're worrying about Charlie," Blanche said.

I tried to be confident. "Oh, we know he's all right."

"Course he is," Wanda said. "But he's gonna get a piece of my mind when he gets home."

Blanche shook her head. "Not you. He's not good at taking direction from a woman. Get Barlow to do it."

"Huh," Wanda said. "Really. Barlow?"

"Charlie admires him."

"Does he now. Well I guess he should," Wanda said.

I was pleased, though like Wanda, I had no idea of who or what Charlie admired.

On our ride home, I pondered Blanche's understanding of Charlie. She must have long ago accepted the fact that he'd do what he would do; it was time for me to accept it too. I needed to concentrate on the rest of my family, especially my children, not that they confided in me, either. Hettie was attentive, but I could see her interests were somewhere else. It was hard to accept, but children grew up; home was no longer the place they loved most, and parents were no longer their most important people.

Maybe Wanda had similar thoughts, because in the next hour

she tried repeatedly to telephone Evie, her older daughter, who lived with her husband and family in Richmond. Evie had been little more than sixteen when we'd spirited her away with Junior Doddy to avoid the wrath of Junior's father, a bootlegger and wanted criminal. Since then, Wanda had visited Evie in Richmond only once. Evie brought her family to visit us every two or three years. I wrote to her regularly with news of the family, and Wanda telephoned, preferring the cost of long distance to the pain of setting pen to paper.

When we had no certain knowledge but felt the need for answers, we tended to make conclusions. Today, Wanda decided Evie couldn't answer the phone because she and her family were out visiting.

CHAPTER 17

Charlie had promised, and I'd stayed hopeful, because if he hadn't intended to be with us, he'd have said "maybe." As our dinner hour drew near, I was seized by a new certainty. Something unavoidable had happened. When Hettie asked if she should set a place for Charlie, I said, "No."

Glory, Randolph and Johnny arrived 15 minutes late, as expected.

"Sorry to be tardy," she said, as I met them at the door. I assured her, as I always did, that her timing was perfect.

Randolph hung up her coat, a heavy fur, and I admired the rose-colored suit she wore beneath it. "Made and given by Virgie, don't you know. She sews for me so she can control what I wear. But truly, I have no time to shop or to make anything for myself, so I'm grateful, even if what she makes isn't always my taste."

"Beggars can't be choosers," I said, making her laugh. I rarely saw Glory wear a dress produced in her shop, but with her gifts of factory samples and irregulars, all the women in our family felt well dressed.

She straightened the jacket, which was form-fitted. Glory's taste was rather conservative, but Virgie loved clothing that showed the body, and her gift hugged Glory's small frame and meager curves. "I'll have to stop at her house on my way home, so she'll have proof that I wore this," she said.

Randolph and Johnny moved into the parlor, where Barlow, Otis, and Freddy rose to greet them.

Before Glory could follow, I touched her arm. "Let's please not talk about Charlie today."

"Oh," she said. "I was about to ask. Bad news?"

"Nothing bad, nothing new. I want to focus on the ones who are here." I glanced toward the parlor, where Randolph was shaking hands with Barlow and Johnny was setting wrapped gifts under the tree. "We need a happy Christmas."

"Oh yes," she said, peering into the parlor. "How wonderful they look. And Piney, too. How has she been?"

"She has crying spells and times of confusion," I said. "She seems better when she's with the young people."

"They're the best looking," Glory said, "and they seem so happy. That Otis! And Hettie, so beautiful. I wish Mother could see them. Freddy looks more and more like Uncle Barlow, don't you think?" She took my hand. Have I thanked you for inviting us?"

"Several times," I said. "Is Johnny disappointed that he didn't get to prepare dinner with his father?"

"Not at all, but he's still cross because Randolph wouldn't let him go out to repair the electric lines."

Laughing, we continued into the parlor where there was a flurry of greetings and exclamations about the pretty tree.

Our Christmas table was covered with the best white cloth, including a second small table that extended under the arch and into the parlor. I lit the red candles, then Tom carried in the platter of sliced ham. Wanda and I followed with the other dishes, and everyone took their places.

Barlow cleared his throat, and we stopped chatting and bowed our heads. "Let's pray," he said.

"I'm ready," Piney said. "Let's have 'Jingle Bells'."

Though our heads were bowed, I saw grins around the table.

"All right, Piney. You start," Barlow said.

At the end of the Jingle Bells blessing, we clapped, and there were wide smiles all around. The children would have stories to tell about this Christmas.

During dinner, Glory repeated her invitation to the New Year's Eve party at her shop. "It's going to start at seven, and there will be tons of food, so don't eat before you come. There'll be music and dancing and treats for the children."

Hettie got a lot of teasing from her brother when she asked if she could bring a guest.

"Absolutely," Glory said. "Be sure you introduce me."

"Oh you know him," Freddy said.

Glory winked. "I think I do."

MY CHRISTMAS GIFTS APPEARED TO BE A SUCCESS, BUT I WASN'T responsible for the choices. I'd asked Wanda Rose to give me suggestions for Freddy and Hettie because better than I, she knew what they liked. She'd suggested Brownie cameras, so I'd ordered those at the store, along with two rolls of Kodak film for each. Then secretly I ordered a camera and film for her and Otis too.

I was always stumped about what to give Barlow, since he'd know about anything purchased or ordered from the store. Virgie had suggested I make what was called a "smoking jacket," a casual jacket to wear at home. She'd provided the pattern, and over the summer I found secret moments to work on it, asking regularly for her advice about the tailoring, lining, and shoulder pads. She'd also decided the jacket material should be maroon velvet, and without my approval or knowledge she ordered the material. I feared Barlow would consider the jacket too fancy to wear, but at least for one day he had no choice. When he opened the package, Hettie and Wanda Rose insisted he wear it for the rest of the evening.

"Uncle Barlow, how handsome you look," Glory said. "Nice work, May Rose."

"Virgie helped," I whispered.

Glory smiled. "Probably more than you needed. Or wanted."

"But we love her," I said.

"We do. And she's in love again, have you heard?"

I wasn't surprised, but I'd heard nothing. "Who is it this time, and what does she say about him?"

"She hasn't said a thing—so it could be serious. Randolph has seen him going in and coming out of her house. He said the man has white hair, and he's nobody we know."

"Will she marry this one?"

"Why would she?" We had to admit, Virgie's love life was as entertaining as her movies.

Surprisingly, my gift from Wanda was also a camera and film. From now on, our family was going to have a photo record of everything.

Barlow gave me a neck scarf of soft wool and driving gloves with a lining of fur. I'd bought Charlie a pair of gloves too, though I knew he'd be embarrassed to receive anything. When we were done with our exchange, those gloves waited alone under the tree, wrapped in shiny green paper and tied with red yarn.

CHAPTER 18

The snow had melted, and a warm breeze ruffled the trees around our house, fooling me into a brief, vain thought that this Christmas might mark the beginning of spring.

Barlow and I were standing on the porch, holding hands and waving goodbye to Glory's family, when we saw the lights of a vehicle turn into our lane. My breath caught, and Barlow squeezed my hand. I tried not to burden him with my fears, but he was always attuned to my feelings. "It's a car," he said, when the vehicle drew closer. I exhaled in disappointment, and he squeezed my hand again. Randolph drove away as Barlow and I prepared to greet new guests.

The car stopped and Jonah Jr. got out of the driver's side. We'd known this young man from infancy, Bertha and Jonah Watson's son, Ebert's grandson, and a friend of all our children. I watched to see if anyone else got out of the car, but I wasn't surprised to see he'd come alone. Somebody in our house was going to be very happy.

"Merry Christmas," Barlow said. The young man shook his hand and gave me a shy smile. He carried a wrapped package, and he didn't look nearly as confident as when he'd helped pull the heifer's calf.

"How nice to see you," I said. "Please thank your mother for the cookies. They disappeared like magic."

"Merry Christmas," he said. "I'll tell her."

I opened the door. "Everyone's here. Come in."

He hesitated. "In a minute. Mr. Townsend, could we have a word?"

The young man's voice was shaky. I felt a warning chill, and not because I wasn't dressed warmly enough to be outside on a mild winter evening. I left him and Barlow on the porch.

In the parlor, the tree lights shone, red, yellow, and green. Someone had moved our wing chairs into the dining room, and in the enlarged space Hettie held onto her brother, showing him how to move his feet in the two-step. From the record player in the corner, Fred Astaire sang "Cheek to Cheek". Otis lounged on the loveseat, laughing at Freddy's stumble and waving off his sister's attempts to make him her dance partner.

Jonah Jr.'s entrance stopped the dancing, though Fred Astaire sang on. Freddy dropped his sister's hand and waived for attention. "Jonah, please take this crazy girl off my hands!"

Jonah Jr. turned red. Hettie looked both startled and pleased. Wanda Rose lifted the needle from the record, abruptly silencing the music. "Hi," he said.

Barlow touched my arm. Nervously I followed him to our apartment.

"He asked for our permission," Barlow said, when I closed the door.

It was as I'd thought. "What did you say?"

I wondered: *Words of caution? Advice not to move too quickly, to finish school?*

"I said we liked him very much, but of course the decision would be hers."

"Ah, good, just right." Had Jonah Jr. approached me, I might have reacted less wisely, voicing concerns instead of support. I wondered if he'd told his family, and if so, what they'd said.

Like me, Barlow seemed nervous. We held each other tight, as though fearful of this development in our lives, knowing it marked the end of our family as we knew it. It was also a new beginning, and of course we approved.

Hettie would say yes. Maybe they'd agree to wait.

THAT NIGHT I WOKE TO QUIET KNOCKS ON OUR BEDROOM door. "Mom, Dad." The voice belonged to Freddy. "Charlie's here."

Barlow and I lifted our heads from our pillows at the same time. "Coming! Right away," I called. "Oh, thank you, thank you!"

"He's in the kitchen," Freddy said.

Barlow turned on our bedside lamp. "It's almost midnight."

"You don't have to get up."

"I do. There's some emergency, or he wouldn't have come at this time of night."

His assessment made sense, but I thought Charlie might have come so he'd keep his Christmas promise. I struggled into my robe and the new slippers, hurrying and panting.

Charlie wasn't alone in the kitchen. First my eyes found Hettie and Wanda Rose, backed against the outside door, their eyes solemn. Then I saw him. He sat at the table, his back toward me and his hat off, revealing a circular crease in his thick dark hair. His arms cradled a bundle on his lap. Two bundles, I saw, when I stepped to the other side of the table. His thick thighs were spread, and each held a small boy. They leaned into his chest, hiding their eyes. Their shaggy brown hair was full of dirt, but they wore clean, new-looking brown plaid jackets, both too large.

"Charlie, how nice to see you," I said, striving to keep my

voice soft and pleasant, because the boys looked frightened. Charlie looked like he'd aged ten years.

Charlie nodded.

"Wanda Rose," I said. "Would you please wake your mother? And Hettie, maybe we should have coffee. No, let's have hot chocolate. Oh, let's have both. And sandwiches. Would that be nice?"

The boys peeped around, curious. "Yeah, all of that," Charlie said. The boys' hands and fingernails were dirty, and their faces were streaked by tears. I didn't have to ask where he'd found them, but I wondered about that old woman: *Jessie.*

I'd never seen Charlie look so helpless. Smiling from him to the boys, I pulled out a chair and sat. We watched Hettie draw water into the coffee pot and scoop coffee into the basket. Then she measured cocoa powder and sugar in a saucepan, added milk, and set the pan on the electric stove.

I got up and set out the platter of ham from the refrigerator. The children on Charlie's lap looked close in age, but not old enough for school, possibly five and four. Freddy, who'd been standing by the back stairway, took a half loaf of bread from the pie safe and began to cut slices. Barlow came into the kitchen, took a quick look, and said a casual hello to Charlie. "I'll be in the dining room," he said. "Fred, Hettie, when you're done there, come and join me.

Barlow had the right idea; there were too many big strangers looking down on the small newcomers. He propped open the door to the dining room. I cut three ham sandwiches into quarters and set those on the table.

The children stared, still suspicious. Quietly Hettie carried coffee to the dining room. I stirred the milk mixture, then poured hot chocolate into three cups.

Wanda and her daughter came down the stairs as Charlie and the children were chewing their first bites of ham and bread.

Wanda pulled out a chair across from Charlie and the boys. "Hi y'all. That looks like a good sandwich."

One of the children nodded.

"Ma, is there more coffee?"

We were all quiet as I brought Wanda's coffee. She sighed in satisfaction at the first sip. Then she said, "My name's Wanda." She nodded toward Charlie. "That fella you're sitting on is kinda like my brother. Her over there is sort of our ma. You want to take off them coats?"

The children responded with lowered eyes and a brief head-shake, indicating *no*.

"Well, they're real pretty," Wanda said.

"This here's Bob," Charlie said, nodding to one side. "This one's Jim." His voice was hoarse.

"Bob and Jim," Wanda said. "Hey, there. Welcome to ya."

The boys leaned back against Charlie's chest, munching their bread and ham, shrinking down into their oversized jackets and peeping at Wanda with suspicious eyes.

I felt certain of this much: these were the children he'd taken from the old woman's standoff. I didn't know what had happened to her, but Charlie's helpless expression told me he'd brought the boys here because he didn't know what else to do.

"We know a bit about what happened, there above Jennie Town," I said. "You can tell us all about it later. Would you like more chocolate? Pie?"

"Pie would be nice," Charlie said.

I sliced a quarter of a pumpkin pie for Charlie, and small portions for each of the boys. We were quiet while they ate, Charlie with a fork, the boys picking their portions apart with dirty fingers.

"We went to Piney's," Charlie mumbled. "Where'd they go?"

"Piney's staying with us for now," Wanda said. "Blanche is in the hospital."

His brows lifted, wrinkling his forehead. "Is she bad off?"

"She has pneumonia, but she's better. She'll be home in a couple of days."

"*Pneumonia.*" He looked like he was trying to think.

"She's out of danger," Wanda said.

"Oh." He sighed. "Glad of that. I'll see her tomorrow, then."

"Sure. I'm betting you haven't slept in quite a while," Wanda said. "We'll find you a bed, but maybe a nice bath first?" She bent down and smiled into the boys' eyes. "Wouldn't a warm bath feel good? Do you know, we have soap that floats on the water, just like a little boat or a stick. Did you ever float a stick in a stream?"

The smaller boy hid his face in the wool of Charlie's jacket, but the older one looked interested. Wanda stood and held out her hand. "You want to come and see if we can make that soap float?"

The boys looked at Charlie. His nod apparently satisfied the older one, who slid from his lap and took Wanda's hand. Seeing them about to leave the room, the younger got down and grabbed the sleeve of his brother's coat.

"Use the tub in the apartment," I said.

The boys looked back at Charlie. "I'll be right here eating this pie," he said.

I followed Wanda and the boys to the apartment and gathered up towels and two of Barlow's old flannel shirts. The boys' shirts and pants and holey socks were crustier than their skin and hair.

Soon the bathroom was steamy with hot water and the boys were leaning over the edge of the tub, playing with the floating soap. I admired Wanda's patience, knowing she'd soon have them in the water.

CHAPTER 19

When I returned to the kitchen, Barlow was telling Charlie what Glory and I had learned in our trip to the old logging camp.

Charlie hung his head. "Sorry to give all this trouble."

"I phoned the sheriff," I said. "He thought you'd take the woman to the Marlinton jail."

"Elkins was closer. She was breathing but she wouldn't come to. I took her to the hospital."

"Maybe next time, think about finding a telephone," Barlow said.

"Sorry," Charlie mumbled.

"We're just glad you're here," I said, because Charlie looked defeated. "So you left her at the hospital?"

He looked toward the floor as he spoke. "We waited there quite a while. The boys slept on a bench. I suppose I slept some, too. Then this man came out and told us she'd died. I didn't know what to do about the kids, so I found the police chief. He said I could drop them off at the orphanage. I couldn't bring myself to do that."

"You bought those new jackets."

He nodded. "They was wearing no coats. They don't know their last name. They don't know anything about a pa and they barely remember their ma. Their neighbors told me the woman was Jessie True. They said her granddaughter's name was Judy or maybe it was Julie. She died a couple of years ago. I'll go back up to the camp and see if there's anything about the family in that shack they was living in."

Charlie ran a hand through his hair, like he was trying to pull it out. "When I got there that morning the neighbors said there were kids but when I called out and asked Jessie where they were she said they'd run off and she was gonna shoot them if they showed themselves."

Barlow said, "And the boys heard that?"

Charlie nodded. "Awful, ain't it? It was scary, and it went on and on like that, night and day. I kept thinking she'd get tired and go in the house, but she held out. Two of the neighbor men and me took turns keeping watch so we could get some sleep, but none of us slept much."

"You did well," I said.

He didn't look soothed by my judgement. "When it was over, the boys stuck to me like leeches. They was hid under a shed the whole time their granny was shouting and waving that gun. When she fell over and I carried her to the truck, they come out and run after us. That was the first I saw them. They were crying and screaming for me not to take their granny. I couldn't leave them crying in the cold like that."

As the clock struck one, Wanda came to the kitchen with two drowsy, well-washed boys in flannel shirts that reached their ankles.

"Thanks for all this," Charlie said. "We should go." He stood, wavered, and sat again, steadying himself against the table.

"You don't look too good," Wanda said.

Barlow agreed. "Sleep here tonight, Charlie. May Rose and Wanda will help you work things out."

I was surprised by Barlow's offer, but not by Charlie's ready agreement. He not only seemed helpless—he looked disoriented.

While Charlie had a bath, Wanda settled the boys on the playroom's daybed. Charlie said the floor beside the daybed would be fine for him, so we gave him quilts and a pillow, and everyone said goodnight. After a few quiet steps on the floor above, the house quickly settled down.

In my last bit of consciousness I had a flash of memory, something important but overlooked while Charlie and the boys were commanding our attention. It was the sparkle of a ring on my daughter's left hand. This image was a much better start to a good night's sleep than the tale of a demented woman's last stand.

~

I SLEPT LATE THE NEXT MORNING, WAKING TO BRIGHT daylight, a faint aroma of bacon, and muted sounds of conversation. I dressed quickly and tiptoed through the sitting room to peer into the playroom. The door was open, the daybed covers on the floor and the room empty. The clock in the hall struck nine. *Nine!*

Voices drew me to the parlor, where Charlie's boys sat cross-legged on the floor in front of our Christmas tree. Charlie stood near the dining room door, looking better but typically uncomfortable, while Dessie watched from the rocker, all smiles.

"Good morning," Dessie said brightly, smiling toward the boys. "Look what Santy Claus brought us."

Still wearing Barlow's shirts, the boys alternately gazed at the tree lights and pushed wooden trucks on the rug. I'd passed along most of my children's toys, but I'd kept these trucks because they'd been carved by Will, a long-ago Christmas gift for Freddy. They fit neatly in the boys' small hands.

"We'll be getting outa your way this morning," Charlie said.

"You don't need to hurry."

"I gotta... There's things..."

"I understand. But first have breakfast."

"We ate already," he mumbled.

"Hettie and Wanda Rose fed us all—bacon, gravy and grits," Dessie said. "Then everybody went to work. Freddy said he'd take care of the furnaces at Charlie's and Piney's houses."

"Wanda didn't want to leave, said she'd go and find someone to work for her today. Otis came home and ate and went to bed."

"And Piney?"

"In the kitchen with the girls. Barlow said to let you sleep. And Virgie was here."

"Virgie?" I couldn't imagine how I'd slept through so much coming and going. I needed coffee, and I needed to hug my daughter.

"Wanda called Virgie to see if she had clothes to fit these boys." Dessie waved a hand toward three small storage trunks stacked in the entryway. "She brought all that."

"All that!" I echoed. Virgie sewed constantly, and her twins always had more clothes than they could wear, but I was surprised to see so much, since she regularly passed their clothing to Glory and sold other things at Trading Days. I looked again at Bob and Jim, still silent and engrossed, then at Charlie, who seemed lost in thought. Or perhaps lost, incapable of thought. Now did not seem a good time to ask what he planned to do about those boys.

"I guess I'll find some breakfast, if everything's good here," I said.

"All good," Dessie smiled. Dessie was like a barometer: if she said "all good" then our duties were well managed, and our household was functioning as it should.

"Set them trunks over here and I'll see if there's anything that'll fit," she said. "If the boys need stuff that's different, Virgie said she'll make it today."

Today? "What a remarkable woman. What a friend!"

Eager to see Hettie, I left Dessie rummaging through the first trunk. I found Hettie with her hands in dishwater. When she lifted a plate, I saw the ring on her finger. "Oh, Hettie," I said. "You said *yes?*"

Smiling, she passed the dripping plate to Wanda Rose, who passed it to Piney at the table. Hettie's face was damp and shiny with steam from the soapy water. "Don't worry, we're going to finish school before we marry. And we may have to wait until Jonah settles into a job. I hope you're happy for me."

I grasped her wet hands and kissed her cheek. "I'm happy because you're happy and because we like Jonah Jr. so much. And lucky you: Bertha Watson will be your mother-in-law! I couldn't have picked anyone better."

She laughed, and Wanda Rose laughed, prompting Piney to laugh too. Piney wiped the plate with a dishtowel, front and back, and handed it back to Wanda Rose.

Wanda Rose set the plate on the stack on the worktable. "Granny," she said, "you'll have to pick a mother-in law for me."

"That's easy," I said. "Bertha has another son: August."

"Mom, August is engaged," Hettie said.

"All right, then, how about Parker? He's like one of Bertha's boys." Parker was truly her nephew, her brother's son, though none of them seemed to suspect. I was the one who carried that secret burden of proof.

Wanda Rose wrinkled her nose. "Parker's awful serious."

"So what? You may not know this, but you're a serious girl," Hettie said.

"Am I? More's the reason. If I marry a serious boy, we'll be a dull couple."

"My dear, you may be serious at times, but you're also lively and fun. You will never be dull," I said.

Wanda Rose looked pleased. "See that? I'm fun," she said to Piney.

"All right, last call for breakfast," Hettie said. "We saved grits and gravy for you, but the bacon's all gone. Charlie and those boys ate most of it."

I was sure they'd needed it.

I sat across from Piney and let the girls serve my breakfast. Despite the power outage, Piney's unpredictable ups and downs and Charlie's disturbing adventure, we'd had a happy Christmas.

Charlie hadn't come to our house that night to keep his Christmas promise. He needed help, and this time he knew it.

CHAPTER 20

Virgie had done a good job of selecting clothing of an appropriate size for boys estimated to be four and five, though many items seemed too fine for everyday wear, like the shiny leather shoes, wool suits, Sunday shirts and ties. But her trunks also contained socks and underwear, cotton pajamas, and several sets of denim pants and shirts that looked right for Bob and Jim.

"Here," I said, passing a stack of clothing to Charlie. "Take the boys to the playroom and get them dressed."

He stared. I stared back. "They probably know how to dress themselves. You may have to help with the buttons."

"Boys," he mumbled. When the boys did not respond, he said their names. "Bob! Jim! You got new duds here. Let's get them on."

The boys glanced from Charlie to the tree, then slowly rose, still grasping the wooden trucks.

"I gotta see Blanche," he said. "Can the boys stay with you?"

"I can keep them for a short time, if you think they'll be content," I said. "You realize, Piney is no longer responsible, not even to care for herself."

He nodded. I wondered if he understood. I wanted to warn him against imposing on her and Blanche, but perhaps when he saw Blanche, he wouldn't need my warning.

Charlie succeeded in getting Bob and Jim dressed, but when he brought them to the kitchen and told me he'd return in a few hours, they scrambled outside after him. I hurried out too, but Wanda Rose and Hettie were quicker.

"Come on, now," Wanda Rose said, catching the older boy's hand and bringing him to a stop. "Uncle Charlie will be back soon, I promise. You're Bob, am I right? Do you know my name? I'm Wanda Rose." Bob peered up at her and quickly back to Charlie's truck, which was pulling away.

Hettie took the hand of the younger boy, who was watching to see what his brother would do. "It's cold out here," she said. "Should we go inside and get your nice coats?" The boy didn't respond. He and his brother kept their eyes on the truck carrying away the one person they seemed to trust.

When the truck turned out of sight, Wanda Rose said, "Uncle Charlie has a lot of horses, did he tell you? He's gone to give them some hay. Would you like to see my horse? He needs hay too. Come and help, then we'll tell Uncle Charlie about it when he gets back."

"Horse," the younger one said, the first word we'd heard from him. The girls walked them toward the shed.

I found Piney in the parlor. She seemed to be fine, but we did not like to leave her alone, so I suggested she come to the kitchen and plan meals with Dessie and me. Wanda Rose and Hettie came back inside with the boys, luring them with a promise of hot chocolate. All had red cheeks and bits of hay in their hair.

"There's my boys," Piney said. "Robert, Ralphie, come give Granny a hug."

"They like to be called Bob and Jim," I said.

She stretched out her arms. "All right. Everybody who likes to be called Bob and Jim get over here." We watched, astonished, as the boys walked into her arms. They stood a moment with their cheeks pressed to hers, one on each side. Then the younger climbed on her lap and the older stood in the crook of her arm. Their response made me believe that at one time, Jessie True had been a loving grandmother. Piney let them go when Hettie brought their hot chocolate.

With so many to feed, Dessie and I planned what would be easy, plentiful, and tasty. Cornbread and stewed tomatoes for lunch, we'd decided, then sauerkraut, sausage, and fried potatoes for our evening meal.

"We'll make cupcakes," Hettie said, looking at Bob and Jim, who'd been attentive to our discussion of food. "You can stir the batter and lick the bowl."

Shyly, they nodded.

"I'll put beans to soak for tomorrow," Dessie said. In the next half hour, the boys watched as Dessie mixed cornbread and bragged about how fine it was going to taste. When Hettie and Wanda Rose set out flour and sugar for cupcakes, the boys left their chairs and positioned themselves by the worktable, their eyes peeping over the edge.

The doorbell rang as I was coming up from the cellar with quarts of tomatoes. "I locked the front door," Wanda Rose said, glancing at the boys. "In case..."

"Good idea."

When I opened the door, I saw Glory hurrying down the steps. "Here I am," I said.

"Oh, so you are. I was going to try the back door." She reversed her steps and came inside, pulling off her driving gloves. "You didn't call me! You told Virgie but you couldn't call me?"

This, of course, was about Charlie. "I'm sorry. He arrived near midnight. I wasn't going to call you so late, and until this morning I didn't know anyone had called Virgie. Charlie brought two boys home with him. They seem to be orphans."

"So Virgie told me," Glory said. "She loves being the first to know, especially when news concerns my family. You might have phoned this morning."

"Glory, I just got up. Virgie came earlier. She left clothes for the boys."

"Good for her."

"Please, let's not talk about Virgie. Charlie's safe."

"You're right, of course. Is he here?"

"The boys are in the kitchen. He went to see Blanche."

"Ah, really? What good will that do?" Recovering, Glory said, "I'm sorry. Virgie winds me in a knot."

I put a finger to my lips.

"Sorry," she said again. "I've been up since two."

I took her to the apartment and closed the door. Glory was overtired, but I knew she wouldn't appreciate my saying so.

"Virgie adores you, and you love her, you know that's true."

"She tries to manage my business. She'd like to manage my life."

"She wants to be helpful, and you know it. Sometimes our nearest and dearest are the most irritating people in our lives. It's because we care a lot. You and Virgie are like sisters, and sisters assume it's their duty to advise and manage each other. They always mean well."

"Do they? You never had sisters."

"I had Wanda, and I grew up with three squabbling cousins, and I got to know a lot of girls and women in our boardinghouse."

She shrugged. "Point taken. Virgie said the boys' grandmother died. So what in the world is Charlie going to do with them?"

"I think he has no idea. You should have seen them, ragged and dirty, and so thin. Somewhere along the way he bought them new jackets. They're much too big; the boys look lost in them. He came to us for help, Glory."

"Shall I meet them now?"

"Certainly. They're a bit overwhelmed. You can imagine—you

saw where they came from. Hettie and Wanda Rose are keeping them occupied."

"How I love those girls," Glory said. "But what will you do when everyone goes back to school?"

"You mean what will *Charlie* do. Dessie is the only one here on weekdays, and I won't ask her to take care of them. Hopefully Blanche will be well enough to manage Piney. But the boys? Charlie will have to find a solution. He's already said he doesn't want to take them to the orphanage."

She nodded solemnly. "This will be interesting."

"He's truly perplexed, Glory. But here's exciting news: Hettie and Jonah Jr. are engaged. And I'll bet Virgie doesn't know."

Glory laughed.

CHAPTER 21

The next day, Wanda got her best Christmas gift—a surprise visit from Evie and her family, which now included Evie and Junior Doddy's little girl Marjorie as well as Junior's young sisters, girls in their teens. Another surprise was that Junior was now going by his middle name, Leroy, and he'd officially changed the family name to Dodds. We were surprised by that, but only because we'd never known anyone who'd changed his name. He didn't have to tell us the change was to avoid being found by his father or even associated with him. Lester Doddy was another parent we didn't speak about, a vicious man believed to be somewhere still evading the law. It seemed best that he remain a mystery to his descendants.

Leroy and Evie were on their way to a small town in Arizona, where he'd bought a newspaper business. I saw how Wanda tried to hide her disappointment. Arizona was a lot farther from us than Richmond.

That week we took many photos with our new cameras, everyone posing outside, because this was before the Brownies had those little flash bulbs and flash cubes that let us take photos inside.

Looking back on that holiday season, I remember there'd been more serious concerns than managing Piney, arranging meals for everyone and finding beds for Evie's family and Charlie's boys. But between Christmas and New Year's eve, I did not hear anyone discuss the newspaper headlines or the likelihood that our country might soon be involved in a war involving many nations. Likewise, our young people kept up a jolly demeanor. A few times I noticed Otis and Freddy in quiet conversation, but they never shared serious thoughts with us.

That year we had a happy Christmas, and Glory gave us a happy New Year's party. All the sewing machines on the main floor of the factory had been moved along the walls and covered with sheets. At a long table, our local butcher carved and served ham and turkey while his wife and daughter encouraged everyone to help themselves from endless bowls of sweet potatoes, mashed potatoes and noodles, baked beans, bread pudding, pies, and cookies.

Piney was happy to see the bountiful table and so many people having a good time. I got to see my daughter dance with her fiancé. I got to see Charlie's boys wearing suits and ties, though Charlie himself wore his everyday denim jacket and pants.

At the party I took the opportunity to have a frank talk with Charlie, who'd continued to sleep on the playroom floor that week and had given us no sign that at some time he and the boys would leave. After a week with us, the boys were more relaxed, but I could not let him think we could take charge of them, or that he could leave them with Piney and Blanche.

"Day after tomorrow, we'll all be back to work," I said. "Which leaves us with a few problems."

He nodded, but I didn't know if he took my meaning. I could never tell if Charlie even noticed how the women in his family coped with all our duties.

"Number one is Piney," I said. "Since Blanche got sick, Wanda Rose has been Piney's minder. But she'll have to go back to school, and we don't know when Blanche will be strong enough to manage, am I right?"

He nodded.

"Then there's Bob and Jim." We looked toward a corner of the main floor, where the boys stood with a group of children, all eagerly watching the piles of wrapped gifts under the tall Christmas tree. It was the farthest I'd seen the boys venture from any of us. "They're doing well, but we can't leave them at the house with Dessie. I can't ask Dessie to manage Piney, either."

"I've been trying to think what to do," he said. "I told Blanche I won't go out to work anymore. I'll give up the badge, and I won't go out buying horses."

"You told her this because...?"

"Because I can't take the boys to that orphanage."

"You'll take them home with you?"

"I could help with Piney," he said. "Blanche said it'd be okay."

"Okay?"

"Okay if me and the boys moved in with her and Piney."

"Oh." I wondered how seriously both of them had considered such a change. I didn't know specifics, but Charlie and Blanche had never gotten along.

"The boys feel good with Piney, can you tell? I think Piney likes them too. And Blanche..." He hesitated. "Blanche has always wanted another chance to be a good ma."

Did he know he'd be putting himself in the role of a father? To be sure we understood each other, I said, "You'd live there, at Piney's house, help Blanche with everything, and be a father to Bob and Jim?"

He shrugged. "I'll do my darndest. I'll have to take care of my horses, but I won't need to go out buying or selling; plenty of folks find me anyway. I might move the horses to Piney's in winter and pasture them both places when there's grass."

"And Blanche has agreed?"

"She said yes, if I give up the badge. She's afraid she won't be able to take care of Piney by herself. What do you think?"

He'd be embarrassed if I said he made me proud. "I think you should talk with Wanda about Piney, just so you'll know what you're taking on."

"Yeah, tomorrow," he said. Wanda was again working a night shift at the hospital.

~

MEMORIES LAST LONGER IF WE GO OVER THEM WHEN THEY'RE fresh. In the days following that New Year's Eve I described scenes from Glory's party several times, first to Dessie, and then to Wanda and Blanche, and later in a letter to my old friend Luzanna. So now, though many years have passed, I know the pictures in my mind are true.

I see how significantly my daughter and Jonah Jr. gazed at each other. I see my son in careful conversation with the girl he'd lost, his childhood friend, Rachel, whose husband worked for Glory. I recall the puzzled look on Charlie's face, as Bob and Jim showed him their wind-up ducks, gifts from Glory. I still laugh, remembering Wanda Rose dancing with Otis, pushing him to get in step with the music. I see Bertha's son August with his fiancée, and Parker on the sidelines, looking like he wished he had the nerve to ask a girl to dance.

I see Glory and Virgie, their arms entwined, watching employees open envelopes with Christmas bonuses. I see the employees' children tearing wrappings from gifts of games and wind-up toys.

At the end of a year it's natural to look back as well as ahead. I remember feeling sad that Will had not lived to see his children grow into accomplished, compassionate adults. I thought of Hester Townsend, Glory's adopted mother, who would not be a bit surprised by her daughter's hard work and success. I thought of my friend Rona Chapman, who'd given me permission to tell Parker about her, if someday I thought he might want to know.

I remember Glory asking Barlow to toast the New Year, and though I don't remember what he said, I see him yet, lifting his glass, that proud, sturdy man. He was my rock. He thought I was his.

I wanted to protect everyone I loved, but I did not have that power, and the future was not in my hands. Looking back, I think it was the Christmas of 1938 that was so different, and the New Year we toasted was 1939.

We had that unique time together. Charlie came home safely, Hettie got engaged to be married, we had Evie with us for a while, Blanche recovered, and the family was happy. That's what I like to remember.

~

You've reached the end of this story. I hope you enjoyed it and other books in the Mountain Women Series.

~

A Note to the Reader

Dear Reader,

I want to thank you for picking up your copy of *Christmas with Charlie*. Readers are everything to authors, and I appreciate you more than I can say.

As an author I depend on you to leave an honest review on Amazon and <u>Goodreads</u>. Your reviews matter. Other readers will appreciate hearing your opinion on the book before they commit to it—and of course I would also like to hear from you about my story, or my characters, or whatever other thoughts the book raised for you. Please leave a review to let me know what you think.

Warmest Regards,

Carol Ervin

ABOUT THE AUTHOR

I've been lucky. Years ago, I wanted to live on a farm, and my husband said "Let's do it." When personal computers were introduced, I wanted to know about them and own one, and lucky me, the school where I taught offered a course in Basic. When we bought our first computer, I discovered the writer's best friend-- word processing. Before that, I could not write without crossing out most of a typewritten or handwritten page, and progress seemed impossible. When I wanted to shift from teaching to writing, the first Macintosh computers came out, and I was lucky enough to have, along with technical and business writing, the first "desktop publishing" service in my area. And when finally I had the leisure to give a lot of time to a novel, my husband didn't merely tolerate my commitment, he encouraged it.

Inspiration for the Mountain Women series came first from the mountain wilderness, both beautiful and challenging for those who live there. I appreciated accounts of early 20th century life and industry, the forerunners of today's technology and culture. When I read Roy B. Clarkson's non-fiction account of lumbering in West Virginia, (*Tumult on the Mountain*, 1964, McClain Printing Co., Parsons, WV), with more than 250 photos of giant trees, loggers, sawmills, trains, and towns, I found the setting for the first book in the series. Finally, I was inspired by men and women of previous generations who faced difficulties unknown today. Researching and writing these novels, I have felt closer to the lives of grandparents I never knew.

BOOKS BY CAROL ERVIN

The Mountain Women Series
The Girl on the Mountain
Cold Comfort
Midwinter Sun
The Women's War
The Boardinghouse
Kith and Kin
Fools for Love
The Meaning of Us
Hearts and Souls
The Promise of Mondays
Pressing On
Down in the Valley
Rona's House
The Years We Missed

A Novella, Prequel to the Mountain Women Series
For the Love of Jamie Long

A Christmas Novella (Mountain Women Series)
Christmas with Charlie

Other Novels
Miss Slappy Gets an Admirer
Ridgetop
Dell Zero
Be Cool, Jule (Romantic comedy by Lorelai Grant, aka Carol Ervin)

Learn more about author Carol Ervin at http://www.carolervin.com

ACKNOWLEDGMENTS

Although characters in the Mountain Women Series are fictional, some of the best parts of them were inspired by women I have known and admired: the women of my extended family, along with friends, colleagues, and neighbors. Many have passed on, but they are remembered with love and appreciation. Like Edna Kelly, an elderly neighbor who introduced me to farm life, and without knowing it, the history and culture of the region. And like Wilda Matlick, farm wife, artist and poet, self-educated and extraordinary. I wish I could have shared these stories with her. I wish I could have shared them with my mother.

Like other books in the Mountain Women Series, the writing of *Christmas with Charlie* was assisted by other important women in my life: June Talbott Dickinson, Michele Moore, and Aimee Louise Ay. All are close friends. I could write a book about the accomplishments of each—all talented, hard-working, faithful, and attuned to what I regard as the important things in life. They've been an inspiration, too.

When I wrote *The Girl on the Mountain,* I had no intentions of writing a series about May Rose and her family. I was urged to continue the story by another great woman, my niece, Jennifer Shaffer. Thank you, Jennifer. If not for your encouragement, the series might not have happened.

Thank you, family; thank you, friends. And thank you, readers, for letting me know my stories have been meaningful to you.